THE SACRIFICE OF MNESIS

By G L Abrar

Published by Lavenham Press 2016

ISBN 978-0-9935784-0-3

Authors Welcome

"Who are we, mere mortals, to place a limit on the puissance of Allah? Whatever path we choose to find God, surely Allah will find us and can make it the right path? Therefore love and respect all who believe in God, and always be open to learn from the faith of others."

The choices we make in this life show how suitable we are to be the stewards of God's creation in the next. If we kill, murder, terrorise or do damage to our environment then we lose our place in paradise as the future caretakers of Allah's universe.

Rather, we should choose to honour God's creation in awe and wonder and to love, tolerate and respect all of "the Book", the golden path as given to Abraham, Christ and the Holy Prophet, Muhammad. "They are your brothers in religion or your equals in creation" as the Caliph Ali ibn Abi Talib once wrote to Malik al-Ashtar.

Facing their death, the people of Mnesis chose the path of peace ... facing a world of man-made terror, may we do the same.

With all my love and prayers

G L Abrar

Tooths Edge
Sea of Marmoron
Hills of Rehish
Fallenmarsh
Plains of
Erionthil
Mt Eron
Forests of
Glaumir
Bay of Estoril
Paraclsmos
Plains of
Abundance
Sands of T
Sea
Heartsease Waters
Mountains of
Serene
Forests of Glamis
The Worl

Mt Bercaliph
Persepolis
Far nest Forest
Haven of Malchor
Sea of Marmosis
Ashland reclaim
Bay of Preduinta
Dustwood
Icelands Bitterfelt
Glasthan
Mountains Crags Spire
Falls of Desire
Barelands Infrequent
Clearwater
Land of Bounty
Words End Relapse
0
100
of Mnesis

SHAA'SHESH

"Dedicated to Laura whose courage is an example to us all"

The Sacrifice of Mnesis

En'archay

In the year 2113, the scout ship Theron launched its exploratory probe whilst in reconnaissance of the asteroid Pallas.

Pallas was an unremarkable lump of rock, the second largest asteroid in diameter in the solar system, the third largest in terms of mass. It could occasionally be seen in the night sky, but only when the eccentricity of its orbit brought it to twice the distance of the Earth from the Sun.

The asteroid's composition contained little of interest to the mining companies who had invested heavily in Theron's scouting mission. This was therefore a routine probe to confirm that nothing had changed since the last time Pallas had been visited.

The probe landed without incident and spent 37 minutes on the surface of the dead rock, returning with one small object. The mission log entry recorded simply:

Asteroid: Pallas Date: 12/9/2112 Time: 01:14

Probe Report. No change to sub surface composition. No life indicators. No atmosphere.
Molybdenite detected in small quantities.
Nesosilicates: Olivine 17%
Inosilicates: Pyroxene 16%
Silicon in natural state: 13%
Hexaflurosilicates: 21%
Carbon including isotopes: 12%
Carbon Chondrite: 18%
Galena, Molybdenite and Pentlandite: 3%
Iron <0.01%
Water < 0.01%
Metallic object on surface removed for inspection.
Silicon in natural state: 13%
Hexaflurosilicates: 21%
Carbon including isotopes: 12%
Carbon Chondrite: 18%
Galena, Molybdenite and Pentlandite: 3%
Iron <0.01%
Water < 0.01%
Metallic object on surface removed for inspection.

The metallic object retrieved by the probe proved to be a box made from titanium, subsequently found to be lined with lead. It was a small box, you could hold it in the palm of a single hand, but when the dust of millennia had been removed, the most delicate metal work could be seen on its lid, depicting flying creatures from Earth's own mythology: dragons, griffon, chimera and the like.

Theron returned to Earth a year later with the box, still unopened and awaiting formal evaluation by the Department of Galactic Anthropology at Harvard University. The view of the crew on the scout ship was that it was a hoax, placed on Pallas by a previous exploratory mission. But they had not risked opening the box in case it was in some way important.

The box was examined within a carefully sealed and isolated environment (a huge air-conditioned tent within a hanger on the edge of the Cambridge campus) at Harvard University by a female scientist. She had been deemed expendable "in the interests of scientific discovery" by her Programme Director and so was left alone to the task of opening the box within the polythene and plastic cage that would become her sarcophagus, should the box contain anything dangerous to life on Earth. She inspected the box carefully and could find no visible sign of a latch, key hole or clasp, nor any evidence of a coded keypad or some other means of opening it.

The young scientist had been fascinated by tales of dragons as a girl. So, out of curiosity, she stroked the tail of one of the dragons on the box's lid, admiring the intricate workings of the alien smith who had forged it. The tail moved, the lid sprung back, and she looked in astonishment at a glowing circle of light held within its frame.

Within the box was a shining disc, some three inches in diameter, which had lain untouched since the box had been placed on Pallas years or eons before. The scientist carefully removed the disc, unsure of its purpose and not wishing to damage it, before examining it under her microscope. What she saw caused her to gasp and her heart beat quickened momentarily.

The disc was some form of record or recording, clearly evidenced through the minute grooves on its surface, yet it was in no language or format she had ever seen before.

Inspecting the box again she noticed there was a tiny slot inside the lid, the exact size of the disc. She did not hesitate, but placed the disc in its receptor ... and then was rocked back as she heard the most beautiful voice speaking proudly yet sadly in a strange, lyrical language.

It took the computers at the Department of Galactic Anthropology nearly two weeks to decipher the recording on the disc. This is the set of stories they discovered.

Chapter One: Al'khaetab

Just over 4.5 billion years ago, our solar system came into existence. The first tens of millions of years saw the planets we recognise in our skies form and begin to cool, such that eventually some of these would give rise to the cosmology we now take for granted.

Those early years were however full of risk for the newly maturing planets.

Life as we discover it on Earth requires many things to fall in place: a planet must be the right size to have enough gravity to hold an atmosphere; must have a tilt and rotational axis such that seasons can evolve; must have volcanoes and plate movement (earthquakes) to generate the carbon dioxide we need for life; must have oxygen generators amongst its plant life and also water on or near its surface; it cannot be too far from the Sun or become cold; nor can it be too near to the Sun or its atmosphere and life itself will burn away.

But, above all, it must survive collision with the masses of debris still spinning in potentially fatal spirals throughout the galaxy and protect itself from the lethal radioactive flares that were very capable of travelling distances of 100 million miles or more, being emitted every few seconds by our Sun.

In the first moments of our solar system, two planets capable of sentient life began to evolve: **Earth** and its sister planet, **Mnesis**, the latter orbiting non eccentrically in parallel with Earth at 1.2 Astronomical Units (AU) from the Sun or about 18 million miles further from the Sun than we are on Earth.

Mnesis was therefore better placed for life to commence than Earth, with slightly lower gravity than ours, less extremes of heat and of volcanic action, its atmosphere forming more rapidly and its surface cooling far faster given its slightly greater distance from our Sun. As a consequence, the evolutionary cycle of life that would take billions of years to see humankind evolve on our planet, took a mere seventy million years before the people of **Mnesis** were able to look to the heavens with genuine understanding and read their destiny in the stars.

What they discovered horrified them, shaping the culture of their civilisation for the few centuries that was their allotted time, before the asteroid destined to wipe out their world would strike with inevitable and unerring velocity at the heart of their fledgling society. No matter their nobility, their constant tranquillity and demonstrations of peaceful co-existence, their intelligence and growing wisdom, their charity and kindness, their love of nature and the integrity of their science. **Mnesis** was to be destroyed such that a wall of orbiting rock, a belt of asteroids, could become shelter for the other planet that would one day be the home of sentient life in our solar system.

For it was the fate of the gentle people of **Mnesis** to die with their planet and let Earth have a future safe from the constant pounding of debris – the result of the implosion that had created the black hole at the heart of the centre of our galaxy, the Milky Way. Even at the outer rim of our galaxy, no planet could escape the risk of collision with an asteroid or meteor, which could tear asunder its fragile atmosphere and ensure sentient life never had a chance to come into being. The *Sacrifice of Mnesis* was that this newly formed planet should become Earth's shield for billions of years against the risk of such annihilation.

Sala'am looked down at Shaa'shesh, as she lay in shock, recovering from the beating she had received that morning. He winced at the first signs of the discolouring of bruising on her delicate arms and the cuts to her pretty face, unused to the sight of such violence. Yet he had known for some time that eventually this would come to pass. Even this prescience, however, did not stop the residue of her fallen tears tugging at his heart, whilst he held her left hand tightly to offer what comfort he could to the silent girl.

Her attendant carer stepped quietly into the room where Shaa'shesh was being treated, not wishing to disturb patient and visitor, but also stunned into mournful silence at this first ever recorded act of aggression by one of their people on another.

The carer was not much older than Shaa'shesh, perhaps eighteen revolutions of their world around the Sun, no more than that surely? She carried herself with the same noble dignity that all of those who lived on Mnesis bore. A sign of their collective understanding that their lives were to be sacrificed for the sake of a new world they would never know. Yet in her eyes, Sala'am could see the first signs of fear, self-hate and revulsion: fear that as the end approached, the civilised world of Mnesis would disintegrate into a place of violence and anarchy.

Sala'am looked briefly out of the floor to ceiling glazed window behind Shaa'shesh's bedstead and beyond to his city of *Paraclemos*, taking the time to admire, as he did each day, its marbled halls, towers of crystal and light, and, at its very heart, the great *Bibliotechnaoi*, his people's pride and joy: a towering obsidian temple in honour of the many stories that the few thousands of residents of Mnesis had told over the centuries they had been allowed to live in this paradise ... in preparing for its unavoidable fall.

The asteroid that would be their nemesis was now clearly visible in the star light of a night-time sky, obscuring even the newly forming planetoid of Pallas that currently orbited Mnesis, and growing bigger in its aspect every day. There were less than two years to go until the nameless asteroid would crash through the atmosphere above and bring death to the thousands living in his world.

Sala'am bowed to the attendant, before asking her quietly:

"Can she speak? I would not add to her harm, for this is already of greatest sadness to us all. Yet I would hear her account of what happened if I might?"

"My name is Kell'aan. If you will permit me to check Shaa'shesh?" at which the carer scanned the monitors on the wall to their left and then bent forward to whisper into Shaa'shesh's left ear.

Sala'am watched the beaten girl nod in answer to whatever question the carer had posed and then her head turned as she looked directly at him, the carer withdrawing from the room by the door behind them, as silently as she had entered:

"Master" Shaa'shesh asked, nearly in tears once more, "Why?"

"My daughter, I can answer this and also I have the answer to prevent this from ever happening again. But in a few minutes, I must interview the man who did this to you, and for that I need to have your insight as to why you were assaulted?"

Shaa'shesh gulped then from somewhere she found the courage to sit up, her back stiffened now with the call of duty and obedience to her Master. She looked fearlessly back at Sala'am, her immediate superior and the person to whom all of Mnesis looked for a solution to their current pass. As she did so, she saw the compassion and kindness in his young face, and recognised the pain behind his smiling expression.

He had been given the near impossible task of holding civilisation together in the face of impending desecration – a responsibility he had not volunteered for but rather had come to him as a result of an overwhelming mandate from the people of Mnesis four years earlier. Over ninety percent of the global adult population had selected his leadership from five thousand eligible candidates.

For the first time, Shaa'shesh, who had been too young to vote at the time, understood why Sala'am had been given this task: **"He believes he can do this."** At which thought, the girl smiled and the room lit up with the joy of her revelation.

"I had gone to the home of a man named Ptere'an to see if any aid could be offered to his daughter who has been unwell for a few weeks. I was greeted not with relief but rather by some new emotion. Perhaps, it is an aspect of the illness that Ptere'an's daughter suffers? Ptere'an himself greeted my offer of help with a red face, with eyes that bulged, with loud words, and then when I stood stupefied in my astonishment, he struck me repeatedly in order to drive me from his home. The bruises and cuts you see are from his blows."

Sala'am stood in silence, his hand still clasping that of his young aide in support, before decisiveness gripped him.

"It is time!" he said simply. "What we must do can wait no longer."

Ptere'an sat with his head in hands, astounded at what he had done, and discovering with each carefully taken breath a wealth of new and unwelcome emotions. His brief moment of inexplicable 'anger' (a word and a concept neither he nor his society had encountered before that day) was now followed by a hollowness in the stomach, an overwhelming sense of regret, a nagging sense of self-doubt and a burning wish to defend himself when he knew he had done something terribly wrong, a strong desire to turn back time, but above all a compulsion to make amends somehow for the harm he had done Shaa'shesh. He did not know this, but he was experiencing the first signs of guilt – again a new experience for the people of Mnesis.

Sala'am opened the door to the room in which Ptere'an was being kept. No-one had known what to do when they had heard of the assault on Shaa'shesh. There were no police in this society, no courts to judge his "crime", no place to hold him in custody (indeed no thought was given of holding or restraining Ptere'an for no citizen would have known where to begin).

Sala'am had suggested that Ptere'an be shown somewhere peaceful and quiet to collect his thoughts, and so Ptere'an had been invited to wait in one of the Reading Rooms within the *Bibliotechnaoi*, guarded by *silence*, but free to come and go as he pleased. The poor man had asked what he should do and been told:

"We do not know. But if you wait here we are sure the Master will want to talk to you. It is to be hoped he can explain what has happened to all of us. But be at rest! Shaa'shesh will heal and she is already up from her bed, having spoken to the Master. She has sent word that she forgives you."

Ptere'an took what comfort he could from their kindly intended words, yet still the pains of guilt and the quest for atonement wracked his mind. As time passed, his concern shifted from himself towards fear for his family. For he knew that by his actions he had become different from the rest of his society and now his greatest anxiety was that he would not be able to tend his sick daughter nor hold his loving wife in these last days of his planet. Finally, he wept.

Sala'am joined him an hour later and noticing the tram lines of fallen tears on the other man's face, once again his heart heaved with sorrow at what his world was in danger of becoming. He had no need to question the man, for Shaa'shesh had given her account and she had never lied. Instead he broke the silence between the two men, with a statement of hope:

"I have never experienced the terrible conflict of feelings and emotions that you now experience, my brother. But I can help the sense of self-despite you feel go away, if you will be guided by me?"

"How?" whispered the other man, not daring to look up into the eyes of the Master.

"I can offer you an act of atonement that shall also welcome you back into the fold of our society."

At that, Ptere'an's looked up in astonishment that the Master should have so acutely identified his need. He became the second person that day to recognise why the Master had been chosen for this task: **"He understands our true desires!"** Yet some lingering self-doubt held Ptere'an back as he found himself trying to justify his actions:

"It was Shaa'shesh's fault! She should never have interfered in my caring for my own daughter ..." and then he trailed off as he realised the import of what he was saying. Self-disgust replaced the guilt that had previously wracked his heart and soul, as he continued more penitently:

"I do not deserve her forgiveness. I have been changed by what I have done and deserve nothing except contempt."

Sala’am laughed.

“You are full of new concepts today, my brother. Who am I to say what we ‘deserve’? Certainly we do not deserve the end we shall meet in two years time. Rather than sit here worried about how others might feel or what you deserve, I ask instead that you come with me. For, I am to give my First Address since I became the Master, over four years ago. I need you at my side to aid me and then I promise I shall give you a task that shall fully atone for your actions today. Will you trust me in this?”

Sala’am stood beneath the gilded dome at the centre of the *Bibliotechnaoi*, the fabled imaginings of his world’s ancestors in stuccoed panels between the carved marble pillars that held the solid gold roof above him. Surrounding him were the many recording devices that would send his first address worldwide to the hundreds of small communities who lived in peaceful trepidation at their impending fate.

At his request, he was accompanied by Ptere’an and by Shaa’shesh. The circular hall at the centre of his society’s temple in adoration of literature was otherwise empty (if you ignored the scores of technicians who would handle the simultaneous broadcast of the Master’s first message to those who looked to him for their salvation).

“My friends! Four years ago, you elected me as Master. My task: to find a future for our way of life despite the approach of the asteroid that will destroy our planet of Mnesis. Today, I give answer to the conundrum you once posed to me. It is not the answer I think you will wish to hear, but it is I hope how we will all wish to be remembered!

“Our technology tells us that the destruction of our world will save our sister planet Earth from meeting the same fate as ourselves – potentially giving that planet many billions of years of life that would otherwise be lost to it. As our planet explodes, it will create a cloud of dust and debris that will form a wall between the Earth and any future risk of meteor damage from the explosion that created our galaxy in the first place. Mnesis will disappear but Earth shall remain, as also shall many of the planetoids that currently orbit us.

“We could have chosen to destroy the asteroid that comes to greet us. This would only put off our peril until the next occasion – perhaps it would buy us an additional million years? But not the billions of years needed for life to develop on the blue planet we can see on our far horizon.

"We have looked at leaving this planet in our space fleet. One in a hundred of us could survive in space for potentially several centuries. But Earth would be the only habitable destination for us, and we know it shall not be ready for life for billions of years. We would be condemning ourselves therefore to a slow death in the confines of space, in the knowledge that we had left over nine out of ten of our brethren without hope.

"We have therefore chosen to remain and to die on the world we love dearly for its beauty and tranquillity. In so doing, we allow the cosmic symphony to create a new score – a new world for sentient life.

"The conundrum you posed to me as your Master was never how can we avoid this fate? It was always, how can we ensure *our way of life* survives this end?

"The risk we face is two-fold: that the oppression of our imminent doom should so change the character and nature of our civilisation that it collapses rapidly and from within AND that in the billions of years between our time and the time when sentient life shall once again tread this solar system, we shall have been forgotten.

"Today, we have seen the first signs that the risks I have seen are becoming reality. One of our brethren, in understandable reaction to the stress of the future loss of those he loves, struck another of our brethren. Now he feels a new emotion that I shall call *remorse* and quests for an act of atonement such that once again he can become part of our society without being seen by us as different. At the same time, I seek to ensure that this is a single incident from which we all can learn, and that this does not become something hateful that shall cast its grip on all of us in time.

"I have chosen to make my broadcast in the *Bibliotechnaoi*, this sacred place where we have kept the millions of treasured stories told by ourselves and our ancestors over the millennia, because the answer to our conundrum lies here, and always has.

"My answer to your question is this:

"We need a purpose to prevent our civilisation descending into anarchy in the last hundreds of days that remain. The purpose I give you is that we tell the story of our people for future races to find. Our scientists have told me they can create a casket that can survive billions of years to hold the accounts of our lives. They also tell me that the planetoid Pallas will survive our own demise and thus we can safely place our record upon its surface ... to be found one day by the explorers of a new civilisation is my hope.

"And so, *everyone* is invited to submit a story of their lives or of something they love or cherish about our world. We shall capture and preserve the best twelve of those stories for posterity. You are all invited to join me in the *Bibliotechnaoi*, for the longest *story feste* of our history.

"Let us go to our noble end doing what we love doing above all other things: telling stories that uplift the mind and provide enlightenment for those to come, with heads held high in pride at our sacrifice, without fear of despair, and the false emotions that desperation can bring!"

Sala'am did not need to wait for the reaction to his speech as the cheering had begun long before he had finished, whilst Shaa'shesh had turned to Ptere'an and hugged him so hard, he had winced, then cried in relief at her acceptance of him.

Pausing until the cameras and sound systems were no longer running, Sala'am finally turned to his two companions and spoke to Ptere'an first:

"Thank you for coming, my brother. I needed the memory of your tears when I first met you to make me go through with this. But now I must ask you to make your act of atonement."

Ptere'an nodded, trusting the Master, yet also concerned at what he must do to make penance for his assault on Shaa'shesh. Sala'am did not leave the guilty man long to hear his counsel:

"I need someone to judge the stories and choose the twelve to be included on the disc that we shall preserve. The judge, of course, cannot submit a story about himself, his own family nor that which he cherishes. Thus they sacrifice their own memories to save the memories of others. I ask: are you willing to be my judge?"

Ptere'an hesitated, saddened that his own family would be denied a possible future in this way, yet also mindful of the fairness of the Master's judgement. It was a sacrifice that would endear him to his society and remove the stigma and shame of his previous action – yes, it was something he would do. Still, he had one question:

"Forgive me, Master! Is this not also punishing my wife and daughter in some small way?"

Before Sala'am could answer, Shaa'shesh interrupted impulsively: "I promise that I shall write the story of your family for you Ptere'an!" at which Sala'am smiled to himself. As that, after all, was why he had invited the girl to be with them also. He had long ago recognised her good heart and nature and known what her response would be. With arms around them both, he laughed as they strode off towards the giant amphitheatre where the story tellers were already beginning to congregate:

"I am blessed by you both," he grinned. "Truly, I am blessed by you both!"

Chapter Two: Numa'mesh

Shaa'shesh sat on the corner of the console table that was Ptere'an's new and official-looking desk and let her feet swing happily a few inches above the cold marble of his office floor. Ptere'an merely sat gloomily, his head in his hands once more, as he listened to yet another story of heroic encounter against the dragons that his people had never found on their planet, yet still insisted existed. It was three weeks now since he had been given the task to find just twelve simple stories out of the thousands being told daily in the amphitheatre below and he had yet to find a single tale of worth.

"We are a simple people, yet we write such ... such ... stodge!" he muttered at which Shaa'shesh began to giggle, then her crimson and blue eyes sparkling, she could not stop herself asking:

"Is 'stodge' a new word? I have not heard it before."

"It is how Numa'mesh describes her baking when it goes wrong. Too much, too fattening and too sickly!"

In the first few hours after the Master's address to his people, they had flocked in their thousands to the *Bibliotechnaoi*, each to render the stories of their lives, their loves, their desires. It did not take long for the many disciples of the Master to realise that he had completely under-estimated the impact of his words and the degree to which he would touch a common chord amongst his citizenry. The *Bibliotechnaoi* was rapidly overwhelmed with new guests, whilst the Eating Halls and Guest Chambers within the *City of Paraclemos* were soon brimming to the point of overflowing.

The disciples had sat in prayer, in hope of some revelation as to what to do next. Then they had sought out the Master, but he would not be disturbed as he spent long hours in communion with the technicians who maintained the space fleet in the *Haven of Melchor,* at the ice-capped east pole of their planet.

Meanwhile, Numa'mesh had taken matters into her own hands.

Numa'mesh was a simple farmer from the plains of *Erionthil* to the west of the capital city of *Paraclemos*. She had lived her early life amongst the vast golden corn fields that rolled south from the shallow grey sands of the northern coastline to the deep blue lakes and mountain ranges of the southern tip of Mnesis. Even though she now spent her days in the city, her early life was always present in the freshness of her eyes, the glowing health of her skin, her tall and slender demeanour. She was a constant reminder of the countryside for the city-dwellers who were her new neighbours.

She had never been particularly good at story-telling; her plot lines remained a mystery to her (let alone her audience), whilst her poems were short and vaguely anarchic. A sense of rhythm and lyricism had somehow passed her by ... to be replaced with a love of and understanding for *food*.

For Numa'mesh was an inspired cook and was never happier than when entertaining with her homely baking.

She married when young to a senior technician at the space port at *Melchor,* her husband being a man respected for his knowledge of RNA replication and believed destined for greatness. The wisdom of those who knew no better was that Numa'mesh had married "above her station" and was fortunate to have a husband held in such great regard by the scientific community in the city. Her lack of literary skill merely helped to reinforce the view that Numa'mesh was inconsequential.

But her husband knew that it was he who was blessed by their marriage and that in Numa'mesh he had found the rarest of treasures. He would look each day at the happiness in his home and say a small prayer of thanksgiving for that chance encounter, on a rare (for him) holiday to the countryside, which had seen him fall head over heels in love with his soul's mate.

He had long ago learnt to seek the continuous laughter at home in preference to the solemnity of the scholarship in his office at work, and to place the loving touch of the free spirit he had married before any aspiration for scientific recognition. Unknowingly, his scientific studies had benefitted from his growing awareness of love and nature, whilst his own literary contributions had become more human and humble, less prosaic, and thus more charming and popular. The serenity of his home life had unleashed his creativity and thus aided him to make the discovery about *Introns* that would ultimately dictate the future of the people of Mnesis.

Numa'mesh did not miss the countryside, for she had fallen in love with the city as soon as she had seen it. Her love was for *people*, she now discovered, and she had always felt both lonely and isolated within the vastness of her family's farm. To have found so many living harmoniously in one place had been a glimpse of heaven for the young girl, soon to become mother, when first brought to *Paraclemos* to meet her husband's family.

At first, she had been accepted for her husband's sake and thus was offered entree to many households by those who sought to influence the scientist through his seemingly naïf wife. But soon, she began to win invitations through her own character and abilities - her laughter was joyful and infectious, her good nature abundantly apparent, she had a gift with children that would see them settle quickly, and (above all) no-one would decline an invitation to dine with Numa'mesh, for the food she served was pure genius.

In the immediate aftermath of the Master's Address, her first thought when seeing the crowds descending on her beloved city had been that they would need to be fed. So, whilst others dusted down their *composito superbus* to place before Ptere'an, she went in search of her hand-written recipe books and began to bake – at first for hundreds and then for the thousands of new visitors to the crystal-spired and glass-towered citadel that was her home.

On the second day of the *story feste,* she stormed over to the *Bibliotechnaoi* to find the Master's disciples still in prayer. Standing there, foot tapping, she let them have a piece of her mind:

"I have food here for at least five thousand and will happily continue to provide such every day, but I need help to distribute it. So, when you have finished your prayers, can you kindly get off your knees, put on some aprons and start giving some food to your poor *starving* people!"

The look of shock on their faces was too much for her, however, and Numa'mesh began to laugh as they hurriedly stood up, catching robes in their heels or turning and bumping into each other in the haste of their desire to come to her aid.

Soon the infection of her gaiety had gripped them all, and in good humour they began the daily task of ensuring their citizenry did not go hungry as they fulfilled the Master's vision.

Shaa'shesh sat listening to the stories being told from the six podia within the amphitheatre, and acknowledged the truth of Ptere'an's assessment. Her people were being far too serious about themselves and their tales were in danger of losing in translation, the fundamental simplicity and humility of their society. She turned to Ptere'an and asked him directly:

"What are you looking for?" then pausing to reflect once more, she continued more hesitantly: "Might it be easier if I ask you to say what you do not want?"

"I am looking for stories that capture our values, our vision, our laws, our way of life. But what I see is our imagination writ large and stories of impossible heroism, when we have never encountered such conflicts."

"Do not look to include our laws," replied Shaa'shesh mischievously, "For no-one has ever broken them!" Then she went bright blue as she remembered that one man had broken their laws and might still feel the guilt for so-doing. Ptere'an, however, saved her from her embarrassment by lifting his head from his hands with the light of new hope in his eyes:

"You are right!" he laughed, grabbing her hand to emphasise his acknowledgement of her wisdom. "For when I broke those laws, the first and hopefully the last to do so, the Master did not use the law to punish me. He found something far more just."

This sparked Shaa'shesh to have a revelation in her turn: "Law and Justice are not the same. Law is the vain attempt to capture in words the concept of right and wrong. But our sense of right and wrong is constantly developing at a rate far faster than the written law can ever hope to match. Where then must we look for justice?"

"In acts of practical generosity, compassion and kindness" was her companion's thoughtful reply, at which the laughter returned into Shaa'shesh's eyes.

"Your wisdom in this outstrips mine, my brother, yet you have also answered your own quest for the first story I believe."

Ptere'an looked up in some surprise and then followed the girl's gaze to look down upon the Forum below, where Numa'mesh and the disciples were feeding the thousands.

Numa'mesh refused to meet Ptere'an as she was far too busy preparing food to talk about his need for stories, and so Shaa'shesh and the judge met with her husband instead. When they had explained their request, however, he began slowly but increasingly loudly to chuckle:

"My wife is wonderful. You could not find a more generous person. But you ask her to write you a story? Alas, she has neither the ability nor the inclination to do so. Her talents lie elsewhere: in the building of a loving home and in the feeding of a grateful family. She has no particular desire to tell of these things, for story-telling is a waste of time in her mind, when there are hungry children to be fed."

Shaa'shesh looked around her at the household of Numa'mesh and saw the clever yet subtle touch of grace that its mistress had brought to her home: the hangings were not those mass-produced by the city's computerised mills but rather hand-stitched lovingly to depict a mother's pride in the achievements of her children; the pottery was hand glazed and showed pictures of the herbs and flowers in her garden, in contrast to the utilitarian plastic ware that Shaa'shesh herself possessed.

Then she looked at the children and saw they were bright with health and clothed in colourful silks, hand-dyed by their mother.

Numa'mesh's story was here before her eyes and it was a tale of loving dedication to ensure that her family lived in comfort and in beautiful surroundings.

"Is there no word that she has written of which she would be proud?" Shaa'shesh asked, at which Numa'mesh's husband was silent for a moment before replying:

"Well, there are her recipe books!"

Ptere'an and Shaa'shesh spent the rest of that day in conversation with the people in their city. They met the crowds as they gathered to collect their food from the distribution points set up by the disciples and they asked them all the same question. They were surprised by the majority answer but it was clear that there was a consensus. Nonetheless, they tested that answer for themselves, and were pleasantly surprised. So much so that they knew they had their first story, though not necessarily the story that they might have originally envisaged.

Thus it was that the first of the twelve accounts to go onto the disc that would be sent in safety to the planetoid of Pallas was **a recipe**. The recipe for the dish that was the firm favourite of the people of Mnesis whom Numa'mesh fed each day, without thought for her own personal sacrifice in so doing, nor seeking any reward.

Blue potatoes

Heat oven to 190C. Boil one and a half kilograms of baking or roasting potatoes for 3 minutes to soften a little then drain. When cool enough to handle, slice into 5mm pieces. Cook one large onion sliced in butter in a pan until softened, for about 5 minutes, then pour over half a glass of white wine, a glass of milk and a glass and a half of cream and heat through. Place the potato slices into a large bowl, pour over the cream mixture, two chopped parsley leaves, four ounces of blueberries and two ounces each of St Augur and Gruyere cheese. Carefully stir until the potato slices are coated.

Grease a large baking dish (about 20 x 30cm) with a little butter then tip the potatoes in. Smooth over the top, ensuring the blueberries are covered, and scatter over a further two ounces each of crumbled St Augur and grated Gruyere then season with black pepper. Cover with foil and cook for 30 minutes, then uncover and cook 30-40 minutes more until a fork slides in easily and the top is golden brown.

When Numa'mesh heard that one of her recipes was to be so honoured, the joy of her laughter echoed from the *Mountains of Pereth* in the south to the *Bay of Preduinta* in the north. As it did so, the shadow of the approaching asteroid seemed, in the minds of the people of Mnesis, to retreat ever so slightly.

Chapter Three: The Pericope of the Orama

Ptere'an stood at the base of one of the Plane trees, which shivered in two long rows either side of the forum in the centre of *Paraclemos*. Above his head, the leaves rustled like the gentle roll of the sea on the eastern sands of his own childhood, and the branches bent sedately as if to honour the gentle attention of this humble man, now made the gatekeeper for the life stories of his people.

He would often spend precious time in silence, taking in the serenity of this place: an uncovered square, flanked by the slender trees, paved in limestone, with marble statues depicting joy, peace, restraint, harmony, art and temperance. His people rarely spoke here, but rather would stand still in contemplation, seeking confirmation of their way of life from the tranquillity around them. It was in some trepidation, therefore, that Ptere'an prepared himself to break that silence.

He already had a reputation for being *different,* following his one outburst of anger and the striking of Shaa'shesh, and suspected his next action would add further credence to the view that he was growing apart. But he really had no other choice!

For the first time in centuries, a raised voice was heard in the *Forum of Faithfulness:*

"Shaa'shesh. Please come down from this tree. I need to talk to you."

A head popped out from the branches of the tree some hundred feet above his head. He caught a glimpse of a gleeful grin, then a nod. He hoped for discretion, as he was already consciously aware of the un-wanted attention that his shout had created, but there was little chance of that where Shaa'shesh was concerned.

In horror, he listened to the sound of crashing through the branches, as the girl tumbled head-first to land in an unceremonious heap at his feet, her clothing ripped and torn, with scratches and bruises on every part of her body from the fall she had taken.

"Ouch!" she laughed, then seeing the look on his face, reassured him: "Don't worry. I am not hurt. I find this is by far the quickest way down!"

"Have you ever considered you might be injured?"

"No!" she gasped, getting a fit of the giggles. "I think I would not like the answer if I stopped to *think* about what I do!"

Then Shaa'shesh remembered that Ptere'an had raised his voice and enquired more gently:

"Are you 'angry' again?"

"I am not angry," Ptere'an replied a little fustily, "even though I am certain that there are times when you would try the patience of a ... " and he paused mid-breath, realising that his people did not have a simile to deal with impatience, before carrying on, a little flustered this time:

"I need your help urgently and I did not want to have a shouted conversation with you at the top of a tree and me standing here surrounded by awe-struck visitors to the Forum, interrupting their peaceful reflection in the process."

Shaa'shesh grinned and the gleam in her eyes told Ptere'an precisely what she was thinking: "Too late for that!" but her reply was suitably respectful as she took his hand in her own:

"Come and let us find somewhere to sit and drink whilst we chat. You can tell me what this very *urgent* thing is that I can help you with. And I can tell you what I have seen today from the top of my tree."

They sat at a chrome table on a glass-floored patio, with the gleaming puissance of the *Falls of Glasthan*, roaring beneath their feet to tumble down the crevasses and promontories of the mountain of *Eron,* on which *Paraclemos* perched proudly yet precariously. This was just one of many places where the populace could regard with awe the wonderful views presented by the city's mountain-top position.

In the far distance lay the two deserts of the western continent of Mnesis. The northern desert plains were of fine grey sand, flattened by millennia of gentle winds and stretching towards the cold ice-blue of the *Sea of Marmosis.* A few tribes of nomadic people had lived in those sanded plains many centuries ago, but now it was deserted, as those tribes had settled in the more arable land to their south ... yet ancestral memory was still strong amongst their descendants and it had been towards the former home of her great grandparents that Shaa'shesh's thoughtful gaze had been cast, as she had sat atop her favourite tree.

The bond between Ptere'an and Shaa'shesh had begun with the shared purpose they had been given by the Master but rapidly grown beyond the companionship of colleagues to full-blown friendship, when Ptere'an had discovered Shaa'shesh was from the people of the desert. For he had been born in the eastern desert, and fished in the green salt-waters of the *Sea of Peredor*, before coming to *Paraclemos.*

So, they looked north and east, to the sensual swirl of sand storms and the glistening jewels of distant oases, and sighed in unison, then laughed at their shared sense of regret, before turning to the business in hand.

"How can I help?" asked the young disciple as the rising mist of the falls left a fine layer of water droplets, as beads of diamonds in her purple hair, momentarily distracting Ptere'an, who gulped at her beauty and then, shaking his head in order to regain his concentration, told Shaa'shesh his news:

"Do you know about the excavation at *Persopolis*?" then seeing Shaa'shesh nod, he continued:

"The Director at the excavation was an appointment of the Master. Unfortunately, S'mon the Governor of the Department of Antiquities has contacted me to say that he intends to visit the excavation, with the possibility of removing the Director, unless he can be satisfied by what he sees that the excavation is in good hands. No-one can get hold of Sala'am so a delegation of his disciples have asked if I can stand in for the Master during the inspection, and I would very much like for you to be there at my side. I have never done anything like this before and I need your help!"

"Of course," replied his friend. "I would love to help. When is the Governor arriving?"

"S'mon arrives at *Persopolis* tonight. We have three hours to get there which is just enough time if we leave now. I need you to be on your very best behaviour!"

Then looking at Shaa'shesh, he groaned briefly, as she had chosen that precise moment to sip the hot chocolate he had bought her and succeeded in getting an enormous splodge of ice cream and a piece of pink marshmallow on the tip of her nose. He recovered himself rapidly:

"You will also have to *look* your very best too, so I will order some new clothes to replace the ones you have ripped. They can be on the air transporter we will use and you can change there ... please try to *drink* that hot chocolate and not put it all over your face!"

Persopolis was an ancient city of the people of Mnesis, which had been buried in the last volcanic rush of a lava flow following the eruption of *Mount Bercaliph*, as it sat proudly in the centre of the *Sea of Marmosis*. *Bercaliph* was the tallest peak in the world of Mnesis, being some five miles in height, and the prehistoric inhabitants of this world had gravitated towards its grandeur. The planet's first city, the start of her civilisation, had been constructed in the foothills of this titanic mountain, only to collapse beneath the seas as *Bercaliph* showed its Vulcan-like disregard for the vain attempts of Mnesis' people to tame their ancient world.

As *Persopolis* had collapsed, some three thousand years earlier, it had slid into the depths, tearing asunder the rock surface of the mountain and, in turn, uncovering the caves of yet earlier ancestors of those who now sought to excavate its remains in order to discover their people's pre-history. These caves had been cut into the very fabric of the mountain, thus surviving the holocaust of *Persopolis'* destruction, and represented the first ever evidence of the origins of the people of Mnesis.

Only thirty years earlier, and quite by chance, explorers had come across the entrance to these caves and trod, at first wearily, and then in growing awe and delight along passages covered with wall paintings – the first signs of any sentient life on their planet. The paintings were enlightening!

There were two distinct styles or repeated subject matter captured in vivid blues, reds and gold that traversed every upright wall and the cavernous ceilings above. The dominant theme was one of mythical creatures, their people it seemed had possessed a richness and depth of creative imagination that had translated itself into legends of dragons, sea monsters, elfs, griffons and heroes. The heroes bore swords and lances of strange powers, carefully carved upon the rock face, and shining brightly to ward off every foe.

Yet, as they looked deeply into the caves and uncovered the remnants of the possessions of the people who had lived in them, there was no evidence of such weapons ... or indeed of any weapon. Not a single axe head, or club, no bronze or iron work save that used for clasps, jewellery and for hinges. No sign of any animal heads as adornment; nor of the bones and carcasses of animals amongst the cooking pits; nor any indication that animals had been used for their skins and hides to create rugs or leather work, whether belts, early machinery or tools.

The second theme was their record of how they had lived. Practical stories of the crops they had farmed, evidence that they had domesticated animals to help render the land ripe for harvest, that they had fed on the wheat, leaves and berries they produced, some evidence of early schooling, even some early lettering.

Perhaps most enlightening was what was absent from the paintings. The pre-historic people of Mnesis had left no account of wars or hunting. There was a single account of capturing a large carnivorous animal that had attacked one of their subterranean settlements in a net and then releasing it back into the wild. Other than this, their ancestors had proudly made the choice to be free from conflict, instead seeking a *partnership* with nature, rather than to be master of it. This ancient decision had unknowingly influenced generations to come and the discovery at *Persopolis* had made the whole modern world of Mnesis rightly feel very honoured.

Two years earlier, S'mon and Sala'am had discussed the appointment of a new Director for the excavation at *Persopolis*, following the hasty resignation of the previous incumbent. They had agreed on a young man, called Eli'shah, much to the surprise of his contemporaries. Indeed, Eli'shah's tutor at the Antiquities department in *Februk*, where Eli'shah had just completed his studies, contacted S'mon immediately on hearing the news to ask if there had been some mistake:

"Eli'shah is the most feckless, idiotic, undisciplined student I have ever had the displeasure to try and teach. I would have failed him but for the fact he is also incredibly likeable. His talent is not in the Antiquities, however, and he would be better suited in counselling or some other role that involves people, rather than things long dead!"

Alas, it seemed that Eli'shah's tutor was to be proven right. For in his two years as director, Eli'shah had seen the number of students opting for his programme diminish to well below the number needed to maintain the tight timescale set by the governing department. Eli'shah had committed the cardinal sin of being behind target.

Eli'shah heard the news of the inspection with a deep sense of foreboding. He had tried to exert discipline, but this had rebounded, as his students had become less and less motivated by the project. He had tried to set out new timetables, to incentivise hard work with rewards, to punish poor attendance, to provide good health support as absence through sickness had begun to increase, and all to no avail. His last pep talk had seen only one student attend, and he, for the life of him, could not remember her name. Her name was Orama.

Orama had joined the project only a few months before and loved Eli'shah from the first moment she had seen him, as he greeted the new student arrivals with his tired induction speech. What she saw was a handsome man, with total dedication to the most important historical find of their age, capable of inspiration, yet trapped in a cage of his own making. She was intrigued and took the first opportunity to look up Eli'shah's academic record. She was astonished at what she saw and then enlightened: she understood suddenly not only why Eli'shah had been chosen for this project but also why he was failing.

Try as she might, however, Orama could not attract Eli'shah's attention. She flirted outrageously, and was ignored. Given she was incredibly pretty and had never before had anything but flattering responses to any approach she had made, this came as a bit of a shock. Indeed, her unwitting rejection by Eli'shah rapidly taught her to be far more charitable to the many would-be male suitors that she would come to reject over the next few months. She also found that she was miserable for the first time in her young life and would cry at the slightest provocation, sometimes for no reason at all, save the desire to have her love returned.

Next, she tried to excel in her studies. She threw herself wholeheartedly into the computer library that linked to the *Bibliotechnaoi*, and rapidly became an expert in the areas she knew Eli'shah had studied. She attempted, in vain, to flatter him by showing her comprehension and respect for the theses he had done as part of his fellowship.

Alas, Eli'shah was no academic and hardly understood a word she said to him, having forgotten most of what he had previously studied. He merely congratulated her and then showed more attention to those students whose ideas were simpler, less complex, and thus more in keeping with his own level of knowledge and understanding.

Flummoxed, Orama concluded he must hate her and went into a sulk. Eli'shah committed the gravest of all errors and ignored that too – to be fair, he did not notice. You see, Eli'shah was short-sighted but Orama did not know that, as it had never appeared on his records, nor had anyone considered this might be the case. He had not rejected her, merely seen her as one rather indistinct shadowy figure amongst many.

Then, one day came the news that the Governor of the Department of Antiquities was to make an inspection of the excavation at very short notice. Eli'shah called the whole team together to make the announcement and to ask for their aid:

"I have something important to say," he started falteringly and Orama looked around her to see the light in her fellow students' eyes gradually darken as Eli'shah stumbled once again over the words needed to inspire them. "We are about to be inspected in a few hours time and I know you will all do your best but I think I will not be with you after this visit ... and, well, I wanted to say it is not your fault."

"Oh heavens," thought Orama, "that will really cheer them all up. Nothing for it!" and she boldly stuck up her hand. Try as he might, Eli'shah could not recall her name. He could barely see her hand go up! So he nodded hesitantly for her to speak without committing the solicitude of getting her name wrong. Orama was not fooled, however, but still persevered, despite the pit in her stomach at this latest sign that she was not valued by her Programme Director:

"Have we arranged accommodation for the Governor? My mother has just sent me a new tent which I would willingly offer."

"He will have mine and I shall find somewhere else," was the short reply. "Any more questions? No! Good. Carry on then."

Orama just managed to escape the crowd of her fellow students and made it to the small copse of oak trees at the edge of the clearing that served as the programme's camp site, before surrendering to the tears of shame at such an abrupt response to her offer of help. She was still weeping when Shaa'shesh found her a few moments later, whilst looking for a good tree to climb.

The air transporter commissioned by Ptere'an was the height of luxury with white leather seats in the main cabin, an oak-panelled dining area with its own bar, an office with direct links into the databanks beneath the capital, and a changing area with floor to ceiling wardrobes, at the contents of which Shaa'shesh had gasped in child-like delight.

Ptere'an had not expected to see Shaa'shesh for the rest of their brief flight once she had discovered the sizeable selection of lace, silks and stylish shoes set out for her determination. He was surprised therefore when she joined him in the office section of the transporter after just a few moments to change. He was stunned into silence when, without a word to him, she logged on to the nearest computer console and began to research the excavation programme at *Persopolis*.

Ten minutes later she muttered: "Oh dear!" and then began to chuckle to herself, but would offer no explanation for her levity to her increasingly frustrated companion. On landing, Shaa'shesh leapt down the steps almost as soon as the transporter landed and rushed off towards the nearest trees, Ptere'an shouting a despairing "Behave yourself" after the departing disciple.

S'mon sat frowning in his personal ornithopter. He had elected to travel in his own air transport for two reasons: first it would allow him to arrive early for his inspection and thus discover for himself just how bad the situation at *Persopolis* had become; second, and as importantly, he enjoyed flying himself as it provided a rare opportunity for him to let his hair down and listen to his favourite music. He was frowning, however, at the report in front of him, the same report that Shaa'shesh had brought up on her own screen earlier: it made confusing and depressing reading.

Programme: Persopolis

The programme has two aims, one publicly stated and one concealed at the request of the Master but of equal importance. The first aim is to deliver a constant stream of discovery concerning both the life style and scholarship of our ancients. The second aim is not to be revealed unless to not do so will jeopardise its delivery. The second aim is however vital for the continuation of Antiquities as an area of study.

Eli'shah was chosen as the strongest contender available for the role of Programme Director because he was identified as most likely to achieve the second aim of the programme. His particular skill set made it unlikely that he would be able to deliver the first aim UNLESS he achieved the second aim. To complicate matters, the Director is not aware of the second aim, nor that by its achievement his true talents will be revealed.

The success of the programme is measured through four key performance indicators: an increase in the area of excavation uncovered and made safely available for new research, published academic theses concerning Persopolis that represent new lines of enquiry or new discovery, growth in applications to join the programme and the retention of students enrolled in the programme.

Eli'shah has failed to meet the targets set on all four of these indicators.

Feedback from student exit interviews indicates that there is a high degree of discipline on the site, with clearly established targets and statements of personal responsibility, and frequent attempts by the Director to personally motivate his fellows. Eli'shah is still seen however as distant. He is neither liked nor respected.

It is recommended that he is removed immediately, subject to your own evaluation upon inspection of the site.

M'ses, Permanent Secretary to the Governor of the Department of Antiquities

S,mon reflected briefly that this was the part of his responsibilities he disliked the most. He was also deeply saddened that the ambitious plan set out by the Master and himself over the luxury of a glass of port, whilst enjoying the views of the deep crimson lakes at *Epitheses*, had come to nought. Or so it appeared? "Five minutes to destination" warned his on-board navigation computer and the Governor set the controls to manual in order to enjoy the rare pleasure of landing the craft on the narrow air-strip just a few hundred yards to the east of the camp site, where later he would dine with his guests before inspecting the excavation the following morning. The dinner was booked as a "social gathering" in his honour, but S'mon knew he would have made his mind up on Eli'shah's future career long before the morning's trip to the caves beneath *Bercilaph.*

Shaa'shesh took one look at Orama and dropped down on the floor next to her to give her a hug. "You in love then?" she asked without a moment's hesitation and then when the other girl nodded, surprised in to speechlessness at the directness of the question, asked her quietly: "Want to talk about it?"

Orama hesitated, but one of the sad facts about being so beautiful and so hunted by the many men in the programme was that she had no girl-friends with whom to talk. She had, thus far, dealt with her unrequited love alone and without the aid of friendly advice. So, she opened her heart to Shaa'shesh, and as she did so, another piece of the jigsaw that had puzzled the young disciple about the programme at *Persopolis* dropped neatly into place.

Not wanting to upset Orama with her fears for the Director, or to console her with the possibility Eli'shah might love her still (in case this was not the fate intended for them both), Shaa'shesh looked to distract the weeping girl by changing the subject:

"I would very much like to see your new tent."

Orama sniffed then pulled herself together. The tent had just arrived and she had not yet opened it but it had been newly bought by her mother, so she was very proud of the fact that she alone in the programme had a new tent, whilst the rest of her companions had either borrowed one or had bought one second-hand from previous students.

"Can you help me put it up?" she whispered shyly, and when Shaa'shesh hugged her once more, the healing Orama had so much needed finally began.

Twenty minutes later, Orama looked down in horror at her mother's gift, whilst Shaa'shesh rolled on the ground, clutching her sides in laughter at the sight of the tent. "Thank goodness the Director did not take up your offer," she gasped and then could not speak again for the fit of giggles that consumed her.

Several days earlier, Orama's mother had gone into the nearest camping shop and had seen a tent on special offer. Unable to resist a bargain, she had bought it without hesitation. A moment's reflection and perhaps she might have inspected the picture on the outside of the box more closely? But had she done so, then the Master's second aim for the programme would never have been accomplished!

Her gift to her daughter was ...

... a child's tent, only four feet long, with two large pink ears and a long grey tail! It was now sitting in pride of place at the entrance of the camp site, clearly visible for all to see.

"Quick we must hide it," pleaded Orama, but Shaa'shesh merely shook her head:

"It is getting too dark to do so. You will just have to sleep in it and pretend nothing is amiss."

Eli'shah reflected that the dinner that evening could not possibly have gone worse. He had stumbled over the names of the alumni selected to join them at the top table, failed to introduce either Ptere'an or Shaa'shesh to the Governor, watched as food and drink were served by unsmiling students, all so afraid of making any mistake that they had become automaton under S'mon's sad gaze.

Eli'shah made various attempts to enter into conversation with the Governor, but on each occasion he chose subjects of academic interest that rapidly saw him out of his depth. Twice he referred to a rival of S'mon, mistakenly attributing his theories as being the Governor's. In the end, Eli'shah sat in silence whilst S'mon picked at his food and wondered how Sala'am and he could ever have chosen such a bore to become director.

Shaa'shesh began to laugh, at which Ptere'an tried poking her, which only made matters worse and so she quickly excused herself from the table. She had seen enough, however, and knew exactly what to do if she was to save Eli'shah's career and help Orama find her true love.

As S'mon headed back to the refuge of the tent assigned to him at the far edge of the camp site, Shaa'shesh caught up with him from where she had been laying in wait:

"Governor! I have a gift for you. Promise me you will bring it with you tomorrow?"

"You are the Master's disciple?" S'mon replied and then nodded in acceptance of her gift, at which she gave him two feathers.

"What ...?"

But she interrupted his exclamation of surprise, saying softly: "You will know when to use them. Trust me in this and all will become clear in the morning."

A few minutes later, Eli'shah headed towards the tent he had borrowed from one of his students at the other side of the camp site from where the Governor now slept. As he walked through the dark, Shaa'shesh ran to catch him up, tripping over a guide rope and falling spectacularly at his feet. He bent down to check she was alright and she winced as she stood up at the long but shallow cut on her calf, before laughing at her own clumsiness.

"Where are you going in such a hurry?" Eli'shah asked with some concern and then recognised her as the Master's disciple and representative, blushing at the thought of what she might think of his poor performance over dinner that night.

"Forgive me Director, but I was in a hurry to see *you* actually! Please don't worry about the bleeding, I am always falling over things and all my friends say I should slow down. But it was really important I saw you before you go to sleep."

"Why? Have you come to tell me to resign?"

Shaking her head, Shaa'shesh said simply:

"Take these and wear them tomorrow. Do not worry about the inspection but make sure you join the Governor as soon as he awakes in the morning and do the first thing he asks you to do!" then she placed something carefully into Eli'shah's hands, before running off into the dark once more. A few moments later he heard a crash of branches, a muttered "Ouch" and then another fit of the giggles and guessed, rightly, that Shaa'shesh had found her own tent in her inevitable haphazard manner.

A deeply disturbed Ptere'an popped his head into Shaa'shesh's tent half an hour later, only to find the girl in a deep and contented sleep, wrapped up snug as a bug in her roll blanket and gently snoring. On the flap of her tent was a simple note, written for him, and typically enigmatic:

"P! All sorted. Sleep well. S"

S'mon woke early the following morning and wondered if there really was any further point in carrying out the inspection? The Director was out of his depth and had failed to establish any rapport with his students. He needed to be removed. Only his overwhelming respect for the Master, and the gleam of hope in the eyes of the Master's disciple, when he had met her briefly the night before, made him even consider going through the futility of touring both the student camp and then the caves beneath *Persopolis*.

He started to get dressed, and the sound of his movements woke the student set outside his tent in order to warn the Director should the Governor rise early. Thus it was that the Director was already standing by the Governor's tent flap as S'mon stuck his head out to enjoy the light of a new day. S'mon frowned then remembered his manners:

"Better get this over then," he muttered. "Camp site first?"

Eli'shah nodded and then turned towards the first of the student tents and heard a gasp from the Governor behind him. Feeling into his coat pocket, he took out the gift Shaa'shesh had given him the night before and placed a bright new set of spectacles firmly on his nose, then also gasped at what he saw.

In plain view for all to see was Orama's tent, two pink mouse-like ears, a long rat-like tail, and the bottom half of her legs, ending in bare feet, that twitched gently as she slept, totally oblivious that she had placed her tent directly opposite that of the Governor, nor that she was to be the first point of inspection.

The few students already awake took one look at the sight and began to laugh. Eli'shah himself began slowly but surely to chuckle, before remembering whose company he was in and turning sheepishly towards S'mon. His surprise knew no bounds as he saw the tears of delighted laughter on the Governor's cheeks.

"Thank you for restoring my faith in you, Eli'shah" S'mon smiled through his joy. "Your reputation for pranks is why you were chosen to be Director here. For too long, our people have forgotten that the discovery of science must be **FUN**, if it is to inspire our young. I had feared you had forgotten this also, but I am delighted to see that I am proven wrong. Now, my young friend and re-appointed Director of this programme, I have a special request for you."

"Ask anything!" replied a dumbfounded Eli'shah.

"Someone rather special gave me a gift last night. I expect that what I ask you to do is what every one of these students is thinking about doing right now, but dare not in case they arouse our displeasure. So we shall have to just show them how wrong they are!"

Then he passed across one of the two feathers given to him by Shaa'shesh and with a wicked gleam in his eyes, headed for Orama's twitching bare feet. Her screams, as she ran through the clearing, chased by the Governor and Director, and still wearing the child's tent (complete with ears and tail) over her head, woke the whole campus to a bright new future for their excavation.

A few days later, Eli'shah booked himself a break away from the excavation at *Persopolis*, for the first time in two years. He returned after laser eye surgery, with both perfect vision and more importantly with a fresh insight into his role as Director. His return to his programme was greeted with smiles by students, jubilant at the inspection report they had received from the Governor, and for the first time he saw those smiles and returned them.

Then he looked across to where Orama's tent had been and saw her, standing there shyly. There was no mistaking the admiration in her eyes and the pleasure she felt at his confirmation as Director. The bridge of love that spanned between them, which had been prevented by his blindness to both her love and his own talent for fun, now crossed the divide to set their minds and hearts aglow for all around to see.

Thus it was that the second of the twelve accounts to go onto the disc that would be sent in safety to the planetoid of Pallas was **the photograph of a tent with ears like a mouse, a rat's tail, and two slender legs sticking out of the end**.

Whenever their many companions and friends saw the brightness of the love of Eli'shah and Orama, the happy result of the burning fire of two merged hearts and souls, they would laugh with joy. As they did so, the shadow of the approaching asteroid seemed, in the minds of the people of Mnesis, to retreat ever so slightly.

Chapter Four: Asostos and M'tew

To the east of the salt waters of *Clearwater*, in the lea of the *Mountains of Esteeme*, and skirted by the black forests of *Velcent*, lay the mansion of a rich and very powerful man, who had been blessed with two fine sons.

His name was Luca.

From the balconies of the tall towers of his home, he had an uninterrupted view of the magnificent waterfalls at the centre of the eastern continent of Mnesis, whilst his gardens sloped down to the grey sanded shores of the largest of the inland lakes of this world, surrounded by oaks and elms, a constant mirror for the gold, bronze and copper rings that circled the planet and the silver stars in the skies above.

One of the first acts of the Master, upon his election, had been an act of compassion for the young of this world, when he had announced a change in the laws of inheritance to allow children to inherit from their parents whilst still alive

Thus he hoped to give all children some hope and opportunity to shoulder the responsibility of wealth before Mnesis fell into the permanent nightfall of its own destruction.

Many grasped the chance offered and claimed their share of their parents' fortunes to tour the world, or to invest in a dream, or to lead a life of continuous celebration. A very few chose to decline the opportunity presented by the new laws and instead stayed with their parents: out of honour, out of respect, out of love. A handful, such as Shaa'shesh, gave their money away, choosing to enter whatever life lay beyond the demise of their world without the encumbrance of possessions.

Four months into Ptere'an's appointment as the judge and arbiter of the literature of his age, the young man found himself being invited as the guest of honour to parties across the planet. Ostensibly, this was out of respect for his important new role, but equally the intent was to influence the choice of stories that would survive as the last testimony of the people of Mnesis.

One such invitation came from Luca, the proud father of Asostos and M'tew.

Asostos had been amongst the first to take advantage of the new law and demanded half his father's wealth as his pre-inheritance. Leaving his father and his elder brother to try and resurrect what was left of the family business but with only half the capital now to do so, Asostos had set off for twelve months of solid non-stop festivities, squandering a huge fortune, before going spectacularly bust. His parties had been legendary, yet when the money ran out, no-one had come to his aid, nor repaid his many previous invitations. He had headed home, destitute, to be greeted by his father with joy, and to be reinstated into the loving heart of the family. Luca had immediately set about organising a banquet in honour of his son's return and it was to this *Event of the Season* that Ptere'an had been invited.

Ptere'an asked Shaa'shesh to join him, intending the girl have some well-earned fun, and totally ignored her protests, her pleas, her brief tears, bravely held back to avoid distressing him, and the clear signs of deep-felt misery in her eyes at the prospect of going to a party at the mansion by the *Clearwater.* In the end, Shaa'shesh consented to go because Ptere'an was a dear friend, though she knew she faced potential ruin.

As their transporter flew low over the *Falls of Desire*, commencing the landing sequence to glide silently onto the private landing pad of their host, Ptere'an, who was dressed immaculately in white tie and tails, with the gold sash of his office resplendent across his right shoulder, muttered once more under his breath:

"Did you have to wear your disciple's working robes? You look like my grandmother in her pyjamas! And please don't pout so, as it makes you look like a mummified fish. This is the party of an important and influential friend of the Master and you are here to enjoy yourself, so cheer up."

But Shaa'shesh could not smile as she looked down on the familiar silhouette of the many-towered grey granite-stone manse below. This night, it was alight with the gleam of glass, crystal, gold leaf, and the thousands of scented candles lit amongst the towering chandeliers in each of the public rooms. She remembered it, however, assailed by lightning and rain, with the fury of thunder overhead, as one small frightened girl had ran from an impossible choice within, believing that she would never again return.

Ptere'an was nearly mobbed on his arrival by his fellow guests, rapidly conducted to the centre of the largest of the ball rooms, before being asked what story or stories he still hoped to find for the Master's proposed legacy. Ptere'an deflected all attempts to influence his selection of the next story to be preserved with practiced tact but, nonetheless, was away from Shaa'shesh's side for at least half an hour. On his return to the refreshment table where he had left her, there was no sign of the girl.

Asostos had waited until he had seen Shaa'shesh was alone before sidling up to join her. He was never to forget the conversation that followed, and remained embarrassed to the last day at his folly and lack of politesse. Shaa'shesh had her back to him, and was forlornly looking up at the crystal chandelier above her head, silently remembering the last occasion she had been left to stand alone in this room. She was therefore in a trance-like dream when Asostos interrupted her melancholy.

"Can I get you something to drink?"

Shaa'shesh turned and smiled up at the young man, his dark hair, sensitive chin, clear blue eyes and sensual lips, reminding her so much of his father. Her reply was courteous:

"Asostos, it is genuinely lovely to meet you again. I am quite content, however, to be on my own."

"That would be a waste," replied the young man. "You are made so beautiful! How can it be right that you are left alone?"

Shaa'shesh hesitated and as she did so, the ghost of an earlier conversation with a man of dark hair, sensitive chin and identical clear blue eyes suddenly invaded her present. The same chandelier had been above their heads, its candles reflected in the floor to ceiling gilt mirrors that surrounded them, such that her eyes had glistened as diamonds.

"Will you love me, Shaa'shesh?" asked the voice from her past.

"Will you make love to me?" Asostos pleaded impetuously.

"No," Shaa'shesh replied to both her suitors, present and past, yet still she managed to smile, for she loved them both so very much.

"I am very rich and can pay you a great deal for your love. I can make your dreams come true and take you to places in the world that will fill your heart with joy. Love me, Shaa'shesh!"

"I prefer to be poor."

"I could force myself on you. No-one would know. None could prevent this. Your father left you in my care before he died, and so I could command this if I so desired. How can you deny me?"

"I deny you because I love you."

Then as the memory began to fade, and the present reinstated itself, she heard Asostos once more:

"Is it that you do it with girls then? I can find one and watch if you like!"

Shaa'shesh could not help it but began to giggle at the contrast in how each of these men she loved had tried to woo her. But she was touched also by the youthful desperation in his voice and so, stepping on tip toe, she bent forward to give the young man a quick peck on his cheek ... her generous heart rewarding him for his determination, but also indicating that she had no intention of going any further than a sisterly benison.

"Come upstairs" he whispered into her ear as she did so.

Shaa'shesh shook her head and then looked over his shoulder, to stare, cast rigid in horror, at the sight of a tall man standing in stern silence behind them both. She gasped, ducked her head in shame, broke away from Asostos, and ran out into the gardens towards the safety of the darkness of the forests that surrounded the *Clearwater.*

She had met her ruin, after all! Asostos stepped forward to follow her, but a firm hand held him by the arm, preventing him from her pursuit.

Shaa'shesh stood beneath the moon in the centre of the *Clearwater*. The shallows of its salt lakes were shifting sands that floated just beneath the water's surface and would gradually circle towards its epicentre.

Shaa'shesh had learnt as a young girl to follow the movement of the sands, her webbed feet and lithe, light frame being perfect for so doing. As a child, she had often come to these waters for solitude, to allow peaceful reflection when her mind was scattered to the four winds, to seek revelation in contemplation, and love in the awe and wonder of creation that surrounded her. To help her concentration, she balanced on the sands, mindful of their ever changing dance, and thus, had any seen her, she looked to the casual observer at the lake's edge as if she walked upon its waters.

A gasp of surprise whispered through the caress of the gentle wind that teased the lake around her, making Shaa'shesh look up in fear, to see the shadow of a tall young man standing on the shore of the *Clearwater*, his face hidden in the light of the moon above, yet clearly looking towards her from the shape of his profile. The girl stumbled, as she lost her concentration and missed the tortuous twists of the sand beneath her feet. Her left leg fell through the shallows and she tumbled into the deep waters beyond the drifts with an almighty and undignified splash. It was about now that Shaa'shesh remembered that she still could not swim.

She woke to find herself being carried through the shallows towards the safety of the shore. Looking up, she recognised the face of her rescuer and she sighed happily. No matter her robe was covered in marsh grasses, her shoes were doubtless being eaten by the carp at the bottom of the lake, nor that her hair looked a disaster area, indeed her hair was in a state that only she could achieve and probably the closest description would be to liken it to rotting red cabbage. She did not care about any of this, however, because all she could hear was her soul singing joyfully, whilst her heart was beating so fast she was convinced she would burst.

The man who carried her appeared at first glance to be either angry or upset. Then realisation came: this was an *abundance of seriousness* that he carried, and she also knew why he chose to burden himself with it. She kept silent, nonetheless, for she was enjoying the sense of comfort and protection of being carried by the young man, and knew that the moment she chose to speak, he would put her down.

Eventually, he reached the lake's edge, found the fallen trunk of a tree to act as a bench, and lowered her carefully. Then he placed the index finger of his right hand on her lips to silence her, before beginning to rub both life and circulation back into her ice-cold limbs.

Finally, he went in search of where he had left his tails, when he had stripped off to plunge into the lake after her, and returned to place his top-coat over her shoulders to try and keep her warm.

"You could have killed yourself, you little fool," he muttered. "Will you never learn?"

"Hello, M'tew. I love you too," and Shaa'shesh looked up at him adoringly. He ignored her, looking back towards the lights of the mansion, where the party was still in full swing. Then he looked down at her once more:

"You cannot go back to the house in that state. I will need to find a way to smuggle you to your transporter and you can freshen up there. I do wish you would think before you act so impulsively. I also think you were very mistaken to come back ... there really is nothing for you here."

"Oh fiddle-de-dee!" laughed Shaa'shesh. "I am not going anywhere until you tell me why you are being so serious!"

M'tew paused. She watched as he contemplated picking her up and bundling her over his shoulder to carry her back, struggling all the way, to the air transporter or even dragging her across the grass by her sodden hair. But she knew her man, and eventually his inherent chivalry took over. With a wry grin of acknowledgement that she had the mastery of him, he conceded gracefully:

"Very well, let us talk then. I have missed doing so, I freely admit."

"Tell me why you are unhappy," Shaa'shesh whispered, now serious herself.

"I think life has been unfair to me!"

"How so?"

M'tew took a deep breath. He was a man who was naturally prone to view life more seriously than the young elfin-faced girl who was sitting before him, shivering with cold, yet absolutely determined to hear his woes before ever she would consider addressing her own. Despite their differences in temperament,

M'tew respected Shaa'shesh absolutely.

There was also another reason that he was prepared to unburden himself to her. The plain fact was that M'tew had loved Shaa'shesh since she had first arrived as an orphan in his father's household at the age of seven, and his heart had been broken, five years earlier, when she had been forced to leave at the age of twelve. No-one knew why she had left, for Shaa'shesh had remained silent on the matter, whilst his father forbad her name ever to be mentioned again in his presence.

"Asostos has just returned from a year in which he has spent a huge fortune on wine, women, music, adventures, the best space ships and hotels, trips of which I can only dream, parties from which few have survived in good health and none in good wealth.

He took half of the family estate, leaving my father and me to work harder to restore the fortunes of the remaining half. We have worked our socks off to bring the farm lands and mines on which our family income has been based for centuries back to the levels needed to pay off the debts created when Asostos took his inheritance.

I could have left when my brother did, but I chose to stay. Out of duty as I did not wish to see my father made destitute in his final years; out of honour as I think my father deserves our service for all the years he toiled to have us educated; out of love as my father was lonely and needed companionship.

We listened for a year about Asostos' exploits, and learnt with dismay that his fortune was running dry. My father waited every night in the vain hope Asostos would return, then to my surprise, he did come home.

Not to work, though. Oh no! Asostos is back to having parties, but this time being bankrolled by my father. Whilst I continue to work the lands in order to pay for both of them to enjoy themselves!

I could have borne this, perhaps, but for Asostos's latest escapade!"

Shaa'shesh raised her eyebrows and enquired softly: "Oh! What more has he done?"

"He and you have kissed! I saw it all. I think he wishes to partner with you?"

Shaa'shesh grinned then stood up and faced him. He towered over her, but her courage was greater than any person's he had met before as she stunned him into silence with the truth:

"I have no intention of making love with Asostos. He is the wrong brother" then it was her turn to place her finger on his lips to prevent his unguarded and confused response, before chiding him gently:

"Hush my love. You have yet to tell me why this is unfair?"

"Is it not unfair that my father should give so much love to one son and not to the other? Is it not unfair that my brother should receive the kiss I have wanted with all my heart?"

"Stay there!" commanded Shaa'shesh and then, before he could react, she had run off into the dark of the night, heading towards the mansion, heedless of the state she was in.

The most important dignitaries in the world, dressed in their finest apparel, were about to have the rare and dubious honour of seeing the Master's favourite disciple bare-footed, with streaming bloodshot eyes and bedraggled hair, dressed in the dripping remains of a white woollen and very unflattering cassock, liberally adorned with pond weed and similar stagnant plant life from the lake.

Oblivious to the spectacle she was making, Shaa'shesh strode straight up to the host of the party.

The ballroom went silent as every eye turned to watch this little girl stand before the tall handsome man with the frighteningly clear sapphire blue eyes. At first, he refused to acknowledge her presence, but she was adamantine in her determination to have his attention. Eventually, he realised that by saying nothing he was arousing the curiosity of the room, so broke the silence reluctantly, yet also in some trepidation at what the disciple might reveal to the gathering:

"Shaa'shesh. In the name of your father I welcome you back to my home."

"Cara Luca. I have loved you as my father from the day that I was honoured to be adopted by you on the death of my natural father. I love you still as my father today. It was the saddest day of my life when I was asked to leave your home, yet it was your wisdom that saw this must be so. For I was young, simple and in no state to know my own heart. Whilst your eldest son was destined for greatness and could not afford to be distracted by his love for me. You made the decision to send me away out of love for your son M'tew and I have always respected you for doing that.

Today I have discovered that your son has yet to learn love is not fair. Indeed, he believes a father must show his love to his sons by treating each the same way. Your eldest son is sad because of this and I ask you to tell him the truth. Tell him how much you love him."

"Take me to him!" was the man's stern reply and Shaa'shesh bowed before leading Luca down to the lakeside to talk with his son. With her own careful words, she had managed to avoid public condemnation for them both, but now she must hope that Luca could find the words to allow for healing.

"What have you done?" muttered M'tew under his breath as he saw the two of them approaching, but Shaa'shesh ignored them both and went to climb the nearest tree.

"Why do you think I do not love you?"

M'tew paused at his father's question, not wishing to hurt the man he loved so very much, yet knowing this conversation was long overdue. He considered how best to begin, before realising that he owed his father the truth in all its directness.

"I know you love me. It is just I think it is unfair that you love my brother more."

Luca looked out over the lake and up to the mountain peaks beyond. How to tell a son he was mistaken in his view of love? Indeed how could he tell his son he was prepared to sacrifice his own love of Shaa'shesh to allow his eldest son to have that joy? Knowing that Shaa'shesh was above their heads suddenly made him realise that only the truth would suffice:

"I love you both and wish you both to be happy. From an early age I have seen that Asostos is happy when he is given presents or has money to spend. He socialises and finds his happiness in the company of *others*. But you, my son, I have always known prefer to work the lands and you have been happiest when you have had my undivided attention, my praise, my company and my support.

I am very like Asostos! I was a wild young man when I was his age, and a great trial to my own father. You are more like my father: wise, steadfast, hard-working. Asostos is the man I was and you are the man I have always wished to be.

I know that you need me more than Asostos. So to Asostos I give money: it comes easily to me and it goes as easily. To you I give things that are much rarer: myself, my time, my company, my attention. To each of my sons I give what you need to be happy. I am not *fair* in this; I am showing my love for you in this, not my justice.

So do not begrudge Asostos money especially as you have no love for money yourself. Accept instead the gift I give you of my time, the knowledge that I am proud of your achievements, and my belief that you shall make a better father than I and be much loved by your sons."

M'tew wept. Then through the tears he said the words that both Luca and Shaa'shesh, secreted in the branches overhead and listening intently, had most hoped to hear.

"You are wrong father. I can never make a better parent than you nor could any son love his father more than I love you."

Some hours later, Luca and M'tew returned to their home, arm in arm, laughing in each other's company. They headed for the billiards room to cement their newfound good humour with a rack or two of the ancient game, whilst Shaa'shesh headed for the nearest bathroom and a relaxing hot tub.

She intended to be many miles away from the mansion when Luca and M'tew finally got around to discussing their rivalry for her own attentions. Having done all the hard work thus far to reconcile father and son, she definitely did not want to blow it over the small niggling fact that Luca had originally sent her away as a young girl out of a fit of jealousy when he had discovered she preferred the love of M'tew to his own attentions.

Shaa'shesh was just relaxing beneath the foaming bath-water and wondering whether making love to *both* father and son would fulfil M'tew's strange concept of fairness, when Asostos burst into the bathroom.

"It is so unfair. Dad and Mat are playing billiards and they always leave me out."

Catching a glimpse of the naked girl beneath the foam, Asotos cheered up instantly and continued hopefully:

"Are you sure you are not interested in some fun? You are stunningly good-looking, you know!"

"I can say, in all fairness to you all, that I have no plans to make love to **any** of your family right now." Then Shaa'shesh could not help herself but begun to chuckle, spilling the bath-water over the edge and onto the marble floor below, as she did so. The water levels dropped and she gave Asostos a far better view of her bare topography than she had intended.

"Out" she commanded imperiously, seeing precisely where his eyes were concentrating. At which he took one last long admiring look at her and then ran.

A few weeks later, M'tew took a holiday and came to see Shaa'shesh in the city of *Paraclemos* for the first time since she had been sent away by his father. The young disciple took the opportunity to show him around the city, enjoying his company, but also proud to show off her greater knowledge of the capital. As they sat on the *Mount of Eron* and looked down on the dolphins, basking in the *Bay of Preduinta*, Shaa'shesh finally allowed M'tew to kiss her on the lips, gently, tenderly, a first voyage of exploration, an adventurous taste of what was to come.

"Why me?" he asked, still unsure of himself.

"I prefer worth to wealth and constancy to chaos. I knew I could trust you in a way I could never bring myself to have trusted your father or brother. But do not get too excited. I am both young and still very immature. I am only seventeen after all, and it is much too early for me to be considering any long-term relationship. I love you. I may even have fallen in love with you. One day I might even make love to you. But for now, you will have to make do with two things: first, I am very happy to kiss you ... all the time if you wish; but second, I cannot possibly make love with you

... until you have learnt to do so up a tree!"

Thus it was that the third of the twelve accounts to go onto the disc that would be sent in safety to the planetoid of Pallas was **NOT the story of a young and dissolute man, who squandered his money, only to return to the love of his father, but rather the story of the older brother who stayed at home, out of duty and respect for his father, and thus learnt the true meaning of love**.

Shaa'shesh's laughter at the look of horror on M'tew's face brought sunshine into the darkness of the lives of all who heard it echoing amongst the *Hills of Relish* and rolling across the *Sea of Marmoris* to the *Farnest Forest*. As people looked up at the sing-song sound of her youthful gaiety, the shadow of the approaching asteroid seemed, in the minds of the people of Mnesis, to retreat ever so slightly.

Chapter Five: Deipnon

T*ooth's Edge* peninsula to the north of the *Hills of Relish* was a mass of golden flowers sitting on vivid green hops of such purity and abundance that the people of Mnesis would travel the breadth of the planet just to stand and watch the wind gently brush the broad hand-like leaves. The sulphur in the soil, a result of the volcanic disturbances beneath the *Sea of Marmeron*, had combined with the loam and silt of the *Fallenmarsh* to the east to create a uniquely flavoursome hemp - a brewer's dream.

Unfortunately, the people of Mnesis had not developed a palette for ales or beers, and thus the treasury before them remained a spectacle of nature, left un-harvested as a natural wonder, rather than the region becoming a drinker's Mecca.

That is, until one day, and quite by accident, some of the hops fell into a pot of stewing rhubarb! The resulting black and rather ugly mess threw up a welter of steam which condensed on the inside of the stew pot lid, and one innocent yet adventurous teenager (in a hurry to taste the stew), ran his finger over the lid.

First impressions were not good.

The young man took one judicious lick of his fingers and grimaced at the bitterness and liquorice-like after taste. He considered running to tell his mother that the stew had turned ... when the first of many hallucinatory dragons popped out of the wall to take a snap at his head. He would have said "cripes!" for he was a polite lad and this one word was usually the upper limit of his exclamatory vocabulary when surprised. Nor was he known to raise his voice, however anxious he might become. Which was all just as well, as to his horror, he discovered that the second immediate effect of the witch's brew his mother had inadvertently concocted, was that his jaw was jammed firmly in the shut position.

Deciding discretion was the better part of valour, he turned to head towards the nearest door, endeavouring to put as much distance between himself and the crowd of uninvited and unwelcome winged serpents that had decided to join his family for supper, and thus discovered the third side effect of the alarming ale: the floor beneath him – previously unknown to have done anything more exciting than offer a sharp shiver of cold marble on a winter's morn – was now rocking to and fro as if caught in the maelstrom of the most violent storm. He stood weaving as monsters sought to rend him, the floor bucked and shied beneath him, his limbs gradually froze into solid rock, and finally his stomach looped the loop before jettisoning his breakfast to create an unplanned and rather unsavoury new mural on the far wall of the kitchen.

When finally he regained control of his facial muscles, there was only one word that could adequately describe his home world's discovery of rhubarb beer:

"Epic!" he muttered and took another sip.

The craze for rhubarb beer gripped the gentle people of Mnesis, and soon brewing had become the largest and most profitable industry on the planet, closely followed by privately-owned and discreet rhubarb addiction rehabilitation clinics.

The brothers Ass'al and Wass'ail had gone into brewing entirely unintentionally.

They were fishermen from a long line of those who had hunted the gentle carp in the *Marmoron*, lifting them carefully by hand from the ice-cold blue seas in order to give them a new life in the warm green waters of the fountains and ponds of the few cities of Mnesis. For, whilst the people of Mnesis had chosen never to kill another living creature and thus avoided eating fish and meat, their ancestry as amphibians still pulled at their heart strings. Their cities were filled with aquaria, ponds, rills, waterfalls, springs, streams and fountains, as a constant sub-conscious reminder of their evolutionary roots.

One day, a particularly vicious storm had stranded their small wooden vessel in a secluded cove on the western shores of the *Tooth's Edge*. They had chosen wisely to run their craft up the sands in the hope they could keep it away from the sea's passionate grasp, and taken shelter themselves in a small cave at the height of a golden beach, protected by a line of trees that bent in solemn submission to the fury of the winds.

The night mares of a black cloud-covered, starless sky turned to the red glazed clarity of a calmer day as the boys looked out in relief at the gift of continued life beyond the ravages of the tempest, and then in despair at the wreck of what had once been their livelihood. Their delicate vessel was matchwood and tinder.

Ass'al walked over to the wreckage. Hesitantly: hoping that each tentative step might allow the sands beneath his feet to travel back in the hour-glass of time; looking for his craft to re-form before his eyes; then laughing at his foolishness as he called to his brother:

"Wass'ail. We need not fear the cold, for we have wood enough for many fires," he crowed but his sibling did not hear.

Wass'ail had seen something else. As the light of the new day had crept sinuously into the cavern behind the two brothers, he had caught sight of a gentle golden gilt-edged glow, previously hidden from their view in the dark rage of the thunderous night. To their rear was a small chamber, formed naturally through the erosive caress of a millennia of waves, shallow and sand-bottomed, but with an aperture that opened directly onto the heavens above, through which the sun now shone in all its warmth and pride. Sheltered from the fury of the four winds, insulated from the cold of any winter, alight to the sun's first touch of every day, nourished by water that had been cleansed by the purity of the surrounding granite, was a crop of hops of such health that the bouquet alone was divine intoxication.

"Ass'al" he whispered, made hoarse in astonished delight and disbelief, "I think we might be rich!"

They took their first barrel of rhubarb beer to the local farmer's market near *Blasthaven* on the *Tooth's Edge* and the brew was a great success, so much so that several of the villagers that day were later admitted to hospital to have their stomachs removed – a sure sign of a good vintage. Word spread that there was a new master-brewer in the region and soon there was a waiting list for their beverage.

Then one day an elderly gentleman stopped by to visit the farmer's market. He ignored the honey, berries, crops and pulses for sale, instead making a bee-line towards the two brothers' beer tent. He asked for a half pint, took a single sip, nodded slowly with one eyebrow slightly raised, then asked to see the young men responsible for such beer.

Wass'ail took one look at the gentleman and guessed (wrongly) that he was a government official, so quickly pushed Ass'al forwards whilst he dived back behind the tent to start packing their bags. Ass'al gulped then bowed and acknowledged he was the brewer.

"I am having a party this weekend and seek to finish with a beer tasting competition. I would very much like you to provide the refreshments and to present your finest keg at the end of the festivities to be judged by my guests."

"That will be a keg of our Old Slapper," replied Ass'al thoughtfully. "We have just brewed some. It will be nicely warm and suitably bitter by next weekend."

The two men spent a few minutes haggling over the price for twenty kegs in total, comprising a selection of vintage Malt n Tar, Hair Curler, Bladder Bane, and Fallers Pride, with the Old Slapper being kept in reserve. In the end they agreed a handsome fee that was far more money than Ass'al had ever seen in his life yet far less than had the gentleman gone to any of the established brewers. Both men were content.

The following Saturday morning, their brewer's dray set off with twenty barrels safely loaded, for a private mansion on one of the select estates in the *Eironthil,* a region of rolling hills, clear blue rivers and orchards of succulent fruit that was the western continent's equivalent of the *Clearwater.* They could have flown the beer, but knew it travelled better on the back of a horse drawn wagon, the slower swaying motion of the dray ensuring that the rhubarb and hops did not separate, thus keeping the nectar within the barrels a rich blue-black colour.

The beer arrived safely, and the two men set out the kegs, tapping in the stops, setting the stays, and allowing the brew to settle. Then Ass'al went to look around whilst Wass'ail drew the first glass of Fallers Pride and held it up to the light proudly. Not a drop of light penetrated through the glass – perfect hue! He swirled the beer in the glass and noticed its head stuck to the rim like glue – faultless viscosity! He took a gentle sniff of its bouquet and immediately retched into a nearby flower display – overpoweringly superb scent! He then poured a thimble full into the planter of a nearby rubber plant and watched it keel over and die – he was a little disappointed it did not also catch fire or explode but still this was a sign of reasonable potency, ideal for a family occasion or polite social gathering.

At which point, Ass'al returned white-faced and out of breath with terrible news:

"We are doomed! I have just seen who we will be entertaining with our beer and also recognised our host. The elderly gentleman who has engaged us to provide the refreshments for his party is none other than the Chief Inspector for Breweries, and his guest list comprises not only all of the master-brewers in Mnesis but also the leading critics in the beer press. They will crucify us for our arrogance in offering them our simple brews."

"We will just have to get them all drunk," gulped Wass'ail. "Half and half Bladder Bane and Hair Curler should do the trick and no questions asked, well answered anyway! We shall call it Bladder Curler."

Ptere'an and Shaa'shesh arrived half way through the party, carefully avoiding the steady stream of medical transporters that were removing those revellers that had already succumbed to the dreaded Bladder Curler, treading their way towards the beer tent, stepping daintily over the many guests who had passed out and now adorned the carefully manicured lawns as a carpet of immobilised inebriates.

"Two glasses of water please" asked Shaa'shesh before Ptere'an could get his request in for some Malt n Tar, then turning to her friend, she reminded him that they were at the party on official business. "What's that?" asked Ass'al politely.

"The Master gave us a tip off that we may find another story here," Shaa'shesh began to explain but got no further as Wass'ail burst out in laughter. "You will not find a single sensible story here, young lady, in fact I would be surprised if anyone will be sober enough to speak soon."

Shaa'shesh sat drinking her glass of water and watched the party around her, reflecting on what Wass'ail had just said. She could see for herself that the party goers were in a high state of inebriation, and she was very afraid for the first time in her life. The Master had spoken once to her of the indications of "moral degradation" that she must look out for in her people, and excessive drinking had been one of the signs of the decay in standards and behaviour that the Master had feared would be a result of the ever approaching doom they all faced. Then a gleaming glint of mischief sparkled in her crystal clear eyes as she turned back to Wass'ail to enquire:

"I could not help noticing you have one barrel kept back at the rear of the tent, as yet unopened. May I ask what that is?"

"It is our very finest beer and will be opened for a competition we shall run in an hour's time."

"Oh goodie!" Shaa'shesh giggled, before whispering under her breath to Ptere'an:

"I need you to provide a distraction right now!"

"Like what?" he whispered back heatedly.

"Take your clothes off and pretend you are drunk."

"NO!"

"If you don't then I will."

Muttering under his breath that the people of Mnesis were not meant to know how to blackmail each other so how come she was so good at it, Ptere'an began to strip off, much to the amusement of the many women drinkers, and to the complete astonishment of the two young brewers.

As a crowd gathered to watch his feeble attempt at belly dancing naked to the music of a clarinet playing a tortuous cadenza, Shaa'shesh dropped beneath the counter and headed towards the back of the tent. First she went to the section of the tent the brothers had set up to wash the glasses and grabbed the white powder and vinegar they were using to make the glasses shine. Next she headed to where the Old Slapper sat in all her glory. A few moments later, she was back at Ptere'an's side:

"All done," she whispered in his ear," and nice view!" she added with a chuckle, admiring his naked backside that promptly went bright purple in embarrassment. Then taking pity on him, she picked up his cloak from where it had dropped to the floor, covered him in it and pretended to be helping her "tipsy" colleague stagger away from the bar area.

"What have you done?" Ptere'an asked, afraid of the answer.

"Set you up with every lady at the party," the girl laughed back at him, then continued more seriously: "A few more seconds should do the trick! Best take cover."

"Pardon ..." but Ptere'an did not get any further as the party was disrupted by a huge explosion, followed by a large black, foul-smelling mist which descended on the guests, all save Shaa'shesh who had sheltered under a nearby trestle.

"What did you do?" Ptere'an demanded furiously and in genuine alarm, bending down to try and locate the girl in her hiding place.

"Blew up the Old Slapper by adding baking soda and vinegar" came her laughing reply from beneath the table clothes. "Now I need to go and find the two brothers Ass'al and Wass'ail and help them find a new best brew."

The two brothers were sitting on the floor, waiting for the ground to swallow them up when Shaa'shesh joined them.

"Cheer up!" she laughed. "I have a plan."

"Go away" muttered Ass'al. "Our finest beer has gone and we have five minutes until the competition. We are ruined."

"What would you say if I told you that I can get you a substitute brew that will be just as good if not better?"

Both men looked up at this, then slowly shook their heads at what they regarded as a joke in poor taste.

"I am serious," Shaa'shesh persevered. "Trust me!"

Then the girl turned to one of the waitresses at the party and gave her a whispered instruction. A few minutes later, the waitress returned, followed by two of the host's sommeliers, carrying a fresh barrel, clearly full of some precious liquid. As they set it down on a couple of stays and began to insert the tap, the host of the party arrived to see whether all was ready for the competition. Shaa'shesh did not give the two brothers a chance to speak but boldly stood before the Chief Inspector of Breweries herself and replied:

"Yes all is ready. But we ask one favour. The competition must be conducted blindfold. Taste the beer and then decide if it is the best in all of Mnesis, but do not look at it."

The Inspector grinned. He liked this challenge. He also had heard much of Shaa'shesh and respected the young disciple, despite the fact she only drank water. So he had no difficulty agreeing to her terms, and set off straightaway to collect together those of his cronies that could still stand.

Ass'al meanwhile wondered over to the barrel and poured himself a taster of the secret brew. He looked at it suspiciously, for it was clear and translucent without any sign of a head, he sniffed it, it smelt faintly of lavender, he tasted it and then looked at Shaa'shesh in absolute horror.

"This is water! Is this your brilliant idea you airhead ... you ... you ... girl you?" then looking over her right shoulder at the approaching competitors, he shouted across to Wass'ail:

"Quick, pack the bags and run. If we are found serving water to the Chief Inspector of Breweries we will be lynched!"

With the brothers disappearing at a rate of knots in the background, Shaa'shesh prepared to face the Inspector and his drinking companions.

"Blindfolds please," she commanded and the host's menservants handed out black clothes to all of the competitors and then helped tie them to the satisfaction of the girl. "No peeping" she admonished them all.

The Inspector was the first to try the beer.

He had expected bitterness and creaminess, so was surprised at the sharper feel to the tongue, and lack of bite, but then the secondary tastes locked in. He tasted the lavender of course, as this is always the first taste to come, and his mind went back to his childhood amongst the cyan blue fields of his mother's village. Then came the heather, a touch of milk followed by a the tang of citrus that made his teeth tingle; next was the taste of the spring time orchards to his south: apples with their blossom (he had climbed those trees to take the blossom home to his mother as she had lain dying), greengages (sharp and sweet, the taste of wind and rain together), fallen pears (sickly as syrup) and un-ripened plums (subtle, sharp and petit-peu petilant); next were the summer spices and berries (cinnamon and saffron, blackberries and raspberries, perfumed, yet dark and sensuous); next was the taste of the loam of autumn leaves (almost the texture of peat but with the added charcoal of the forest fire); next came the winter's gift (the scent of pine that cleansed the lungs and the touch of acid freshening the tongue); and finally, the pure power of the ancient granite (adding its gentle effervescence).

"My goodness that is good," he muttered. "This beer has such a deep history, it is without doubt the emperor of all brews." At which, Shaa'shesh kissed him on the cheek and then removed his blindfold.

The Inspector looked at his glass and frowned briefly at the clarity of the liquid before him, but Shaa'shesh was ready for his unvoiced question:

"We call it *Clear Beer*," at which he nodded wisely and then watched as his colleagues enjoyed their own first taste of this master beer. The competition was never in doubt. All agreed that Clear Beer was a worthy winner of the award of being the Supreme Ale of the Era, whilst Ass'al and Wass'ail were declared Master Brewers in their absence.

"They are very shy!" Shaa'shesh twinkled at the Inspector, "but I promise to tell them about the award."

"Make sure they know we must have more of this beer. When word gets round, I think it will prove to be the most popular drink in our world. Now are you sure you will not join me in a glass? It would make an old man very happy if you did."

Holding his hand, she smiled up at him:

"Perhaps *just this once* I might. It is, after all, such a special brew."

Over the ensuing months, more and more people converted to the new Clear

Beer produced by Ass'al and Wass'ail. Thus it was that the fourth of the twelve accounts to go onto the disc that would be sent in safety to the planetoid of Pallas was **the story of water that turned into beer and beer that turned into water.**

As people began to commune once more with the taste of the fresh waters from their springs, lakes and rivers, turning their backs on the rhubarb beer that had begun to cloud their appreciation of the natural world, the shadow of the approaching asteroid seemed, in the minds of the people of Mnesis, to retreat ever so slightly.

Chapter Six: Shemer

The woodland region of *Samarriyun* sat at the very southern most point of the *Forests of Glamis*, a peaceful area, rarely disturbed by visitors, and famous for little except the inherent generosity of spirit of its people. For once upon a time, a stranger had been the unfortunate victim of an attack by a wild boar, and, severely gored, had been left by several other travellers until rescued by a good Samriyan. From that moment onwards the Samriyan's earned the respect of the people of Mnesis for their unselfish aid, though alas they also retained a reputation for simplicity of mind that was totally undeserved, yet often the lot of the kind-hearted.

Ptere'an sat on Shaa'shesh's balcony, in a rather fetching pink dressing gown, reading the daily newspaper, whilst occasionally picking at the scant breakfast she had prepared for them both.

He had crashed out in her apartment after a long night of debating the merits of several tracts and scripts, lengthy discussions which would easily have continued long into the early hours had not Ptere'an eventually surrendered to the desire to sleep.

Too tired to make it back to his own rooms in the *Praesidia*, the complex for senior functionaries in the Governing Body of Mnesis, he had woken Shaa'shesh up in her small apartment by the *Bibliotechnaoi* and deposited himself on the couch in her reading room. It was a sign of the strength of their friendship that she had not batted an eyelid, merely gone to find him a blanket and the dressing gown he now wore.

Shaa'shesh looked across the breakfast table and tried desperately to frown but the sight of her friend in her pink dressing gown merely saw her dissolve into hoots of laughter – which Ptere'an ignored with great superiority. Shaa'shesh was irritated though by the presence of a newspaper. For the production of paper was an act of murder in her eyes, requiring the death of many of her friends, her beloved trees. Eventually Ptere'an looked up from his journal and noticed that the girl was strangely subdued. He asked her kindly:

"Alright. What is up?"

"I do not like newspapers," she replied sadly "yet I suppose you must read them?"

"I do not have to read them in front of you," he replied, folding the paper away and placing it out of sight beneath the table. He was heartened by her grin in response and, emboldened, decided to tell her what he had just read:

"Actually, the article I was looking at is very interesting. It follows a letter from a young lady in *Samarriyun,* and given your interest in signs of *moral degradation* amongst our people, I think you may want to look into this?"

"Nothing will make me read a newspaper!" the girl retorted with some pique, but Ptere'an could see that her curiosity was aroused, and taking pity on her, he offered to summarise the letter and the article from memory:

"After all, it is a good story I think, though sad in its ending."

Shaa'shesh listened attentively and as she did so the unhappy revelation came to her that this was indeed another sign of that which the Master had feared. Ptere'an's account began with the letter to the editor the previous day:

"Yesterday, an elderly lady from the region of *Samarriyun*, wrote to express her concern that the acts of kindness for which her people are so well-known were in danger of becoming a thing of the past. There is a new fad amongst our young: to play japes on their elders and those who are vulnerable. No longer for fun, but rather something much more cruel has begun to develop – the tricks are designed to ridicule that which once we might respect. This new phenomenon is doubtless the result of a combination of boredom and fear for the future, yet it is hard to understand or justify.

"It seems four days ago, a group of youths pretended that one of their number was drowning in a lake and thus persuaded a passing *Samriyan* farm girl called Shemer, smartly dressed to go to the local mosque, to dive into the waters at risk of her own life. The girl nearly drowned in her attempt to bring to the shore the man she believed to be in danger, slipping in the mud in her high heels, and is still recovering in the local medical centre. Alas, the whole thing was a hoax and the group of lads left the girl half-dead, making off in hoots of laughter at their nearly tragic trickery.

"The letter is disturbing however as it goes on to say that in the current climate of tom-foolery and buffoonery, no-one should risk coming to the aid of a stranger. The editorial later in the same paper agrees with this, saying only the truly unwise or naïf would put their own life at risk in the way that Shemer did."

Shaa'shesh sat quietly for a moment, deep in thought, and then slowly began to laugh, her delight in what she had heard unfolding like the petals of the wakening rose:

"This is not the end of the story, my friend, but merely the beginning. Let us see what Shemer does when she wakes up."

"Shall we go to hear her story then?" Ptere'an enquired, not doubting for a moment Shaa'shesh's insight as he had long ago learned to trust the girl's instincts in such things.

"It pains me to say this, and do not crow at my inconsistency, but let us wait for next week's paper and I hope that all will become clear. I still do not like newspapers ... but I confess that I am hooked by this story."

Shemer woke in some pain and would have cried out, but then the memory of her ordeal returned, flooding her recovering senses with the pain and distress of her fall into the lake, where she had attempted to rescue a young man in clear jeopardy. She let her mind drift towards the epicentre of pain in her left leg, feeling the cold and implacable grasp of the plaster that held her thigh immobilised as it healed. She grimaced ruefully, as she realised her femur must have been broken in the recklessness of her dive into the deep waters of an unfamiliar lake.

Shemer was not the best of swimmers, nor particularly adventurous. Courage was not regarded as part of her repertoire, and for the life of her, she could not think why she had decided to plunge into the dark waters ... but then she recalled the look of fear on the face of the young man, trying desperately to stay afloat in the icy grip of the shadowy depths. His honest pleading beautiful brown eyes had drawn her in, to her own cost.

Suddenly she wept as the realisation came that she must have failed in her rescue attempt: the man had drowned for certain, and it was her fault. Her feebleness, her inability to swim, her foolishness in diving into shallow waters had all led to his unnecessary death. In her newfound anxiety, her blood pressure began to rise alarmingly and a klaxon went off on the nurse attendant's console in the main atrium of the medical centre. A few moments later, a concerned member of staff put her head around the door of Shemer's room, took one look at the poor girl weeping uncontrollably, and walked across to her bedside to hold her hand in comfort:

"My name is Ky'maan. Talk to me if it will help."

Shemer gave a loud sniff and then tugged at the warm hand of her companion gratefully, drawing relief from her calm presence.

"He died?" she whispered part question, part plea, packaged in an outpouring of remorse and regret.

Ky'maan hesitated, not knowing how to begin to describe to this generous soul before her, the true horror of what had happened. In the end, she went for clinical simplicity, hoping the starkness of her account would shock the girl out of her self-pity.

"His name is LeMorc and he lives. All that has been done by him and his companions was to trick you into to diving into the lake. He sought to make mockery of your kindness and, in so doing, nearly killed you. Yet, even when this became apparent, he left you to die and ran off in laughter."

Shemer sat rigid in silence. She genuinely did not understand what was being said. She could conceive of "a trick" of course: for this is something her people would do for fun to make each other laugh. She could recall the conjurations of her father when she was a child and the great delight she had felt when he would produce a penny from behind her ear or down her nose, for example.

But to trick someone into injuring themselves was a new concept, and then to leave them behind was so implausible that she considered whether it was Ky'maan who now played the trick? Yet she could not find any humour at all in what was being said by the attendant and thus came the realisation that she was being told the truth. With this came the revelation that she had been the victim of an action so very terrible that her remorseful tears began to flow once more. This time she cried for her people's loss of honour. Her own harm was nothing in her mind to the unwitting damage done to the psyche of her world.

"Rather I had never lived than I allow this to happen to me! Better that I should have had the intelligence to see through the trick than I become the victim of such cruelty."

"Nonsense," replied Ky'maan tartly, tapping in the code on the bedside console to pump Shemer full of tranquillisers, knocking her out before she could be guilty of saying any more such idiocy.

The following morning Shemer lifted herself carefully into the carved ash crutches that would be her trusty support for the next few weeks, whilst her shattered femur began the slow but inexorable process of self-repair.

The break had been clean and would heal in good time, provided Shemer did "nothing else foolish" had muttered her physician as she had left the medical centre and limped off towards her farm on the distant banks of the river *Flerin*.

Shemer silently shrugged off all offers of aid, as she very much wanted to be alone: to contemplate the sad state of affairs that her act of gullible generosity had precipitated. Eventually she came to the shores of the lake, where only a few days before her innocence had misled her into an action of rescue that she now feared would unravel centuries of selflessness by her people. She knelt by the waters, lowering herself stiffly and unsteadily into their cold and bitter grasp, and prayed.

LeMorc could not believe his luck. The girl had returned, alone, and now he could trick her once more. "Did she enjoy being made a fool?" he wondered. He might be alone this time, without the aid of his friends, but he already knew the girl was crippled and unable to swim. He would push her in and watch her flounder. Perhaps he might rescue her if she pleaded with him? But he would rid her once and for all of her unbearable and totally boring desire to help others. "By what right did she save those who were already doomed?" he screamed inside, whilst treading carefully amongst the rocks in order to reach her vulnerable back undetected.

One thin strand of lichen was his undoing. His angry eyes burning into the back of Shemer's head, he did not spot it until his foot had started to slide on its sheer surface. He slipped, he cried out and he fell, to land head first against the sharpness of the black rocks that lay beneath the smooth surface of the languid lake. Stunned, and slowly sinking to a watery death, he held out one hand in vain hope, and felt the thud of ash strike his palm.

Shemer had seen a glimpse of the man, then heard the splash and immediately stood, nearly falling in herself, to see what she could do. It took her less than a second to recognise the face of the man whose taunting trick had destroyed the peace of her own mind, and even less than that to realise what she must now do. She grabbed her stick and swung it at him:

"Take it!"

"Never!" he whispered and pulled his hand away.

Shemer did not hesitate but casting her crutches to one side, she flung herself into the water besides him.

"Take my life then" she laughed without bitterness and began to sink beneath him as the water filled the plaster cast around her leg and its weight dragged her to the rocks at his feet, to provide the precious purchase for him to step from the slippery slopes of the smooth granite on the bed of the lake.

At last the shadowy dream of spite that had gripped LeMorc for days lifted to allow the brightness of love, hope and respect to return. Fear for the girl drove the fog and paralysation of his own pain into the distant recesses of his mind, to be replaced with the rush of realisation that nothing he would do could ever stop Shemer from her desire to help him. His own healing became complete as, through the dark horrors of remembering his own previous petty actions, he had the final revelation that this was his only chance to rescue a self-effacing spirit whose one driving desire had ever and always been to come to his own relief.

With all his might, he drove his right arm deep into the waters until he could feel the swirling tendrils of her hair, took a careful grip on a handful of her meandering mane, and then pulled with all his might until her face burst to the surface. She coughed once, spluttered and then spat out some weed, before giving an almighty grin:

"If we are both going to keep playing tricks on each other then we really do need to learn to swim better!"

At which LeMorc joined in her laughter, at first ruefully, but then with growing delight as he understood he had found something far greater than the fun of playing a cruel trick on the girl:

"I will always look to trick you if I can count on you to rescue me ... but never again will I let you come to any harm" he said humbly.

The next day, the newspapers carried the account of Shemer's rescue of LeMorc. It continued with the news of the couple reporting to the local Government building, so that the young man might be punished for his prior and nearly fatal trick on the girl. Shemer's tormentor had stood unwavering, waiting for the deliberation of the disciple whose appointed role was to administer to this remote and bucolic province. The young man was unbowed by the prospect of any punishment. The disciple, on the other hand, was totally unprepared for this eventuality, having never been asked to punish anyone before in his life, and so turned to Shemer in despair to ask:

"What shall I do?"

"Have no fear, sir. I have just the punishment for him!"

So, they were married. And in those final days of the world of Mnesis, they lived together, tending her fields and crops and husbanding her many herds. She would often fall, as her crutches would slip in the sheen of the grassy fields, but he was always there to rescue her, with those dark brown eyes that had completely captured her heart, that first time he had pleaded for his life in the cold waters of her lake.

"How did you know?" asked Ptere'an, smiling as he read the news that once more the people of *Samarriyun* had shaken off their self doubt over the trickery of a small minority of their youth, and could be expected to come to the rescue of any and all passing strangers.

Shaa'shesh looked out towards the rising sun, as it bled its crimson rays over the blue sea in the bay below, and thought wistfully of M'tew:

"You must really love someone to dive in to a lake to save them *with your best high heels still on*! Had LeMorc been just some handsome stranger, Shemer would have stopped to take her shoes off. But she had already fallen in love with those dark eyes of his, and thus given up all hope of her own life to try and save his. I merely wished that her love would win through and I was right ... as I hope my own love will be victorious too one day."

Thus it was that the fifth of the twelve accounts to go onto the disc that would be sent in safety to the planetoid of Pallas was **the newspaper article, complete with a sticky stain of dark brown marmalade, about the good farm-hand from Samarriyun who rescued her lover from his own self despite.**

Shaa'shesh's laughter at Ptere'an's exasperation as she explained how she had known that Shemer was in love was heard as far as the charmed couple standing at the green arched entrance to the *Forests of Glamis*. LeMorc and Shemer's shared smile of joy in happy response to the young disciple's delight, drove the shadows of the approaching asteroid, in the minds of the people of Mnesis, ever further into the distance.

Chapter Seven: The Turbulent Turbot

No-one could remember how the timber framed cottage, standing proudly on the cliffs above the crimsons sands of the *Sea of Bashfulness*, had earned its name as the *Turbulent Turbot* (no-one that is save for Shaa'shesh).

The *Turbulent Turbot* was a place of fond memories for those who had once sailed the wild seas that battered the green limes-wold and hugged the swirling beaches of the former fishing fleets of Mnesis, whose colourful sails and glass mooring buoys, had reflected upon the night-time water in a chequer-board of bubbling bright brilliance in the bay below.

Once, the harbour beneath the comfort of the *Turbulent Turbot*, with its cosy log fires, soft battered leather sofas, curling leather bound books of antiquity in their crooked pine bookcases, accompanied by the aroma of the most pungent of coffees and spices, had seethed with the industry of sea farers from across the western continent. But the days when those who fished were held in the highest regard: for their adventures, their voyages of discovery, their stories of mythical creatures and lands, had long since receded before the advent of more rapid transportation than the simple barques and schooners of those who had lived by, with and for the sea.

A few, inspired by the whisper of the waves and the imponderability of the depths, continued to revere the *Revelation of the Sea*, and to ponder on the secrets that each encounter with the brutality of such untamed waters would uncover *within themselves* as much as before their eyes.

One such revenant was Shaa'shesh, who may never have learnt to swim, but whose child-like addiction to the sound of the sea drew her each year to return to the quiet haven of the

Turbulent Turbot and watch through its lead-glazed windows as the proud crests of the giant waves that had traversed the ocean beyond the sea would strike with hungry ferocity, tearing away yet another layer of the limestone upon which the near-deserted pub perched perilously yet defiantly. When no-one was looking, and indeed there were very few to look that day, she would stick her tongue out at the waves, daring them to find her in the safety and warmth of the bench on which she sat, a pitcher of water and a cheese sandwich as her companions.

That the people of Mnesis should have taken up fishing at all was a mystery. From the very beginnings of their culture, as attested by their most ancient of histories and from the studies of their pre-history, this gentle people had turned their back on the slaying of any other living creature, to become a civilisation for whom the eating of meat or fish was an abhorrence. Yet the sea had drawn them to the challenge of its exploration and conquest, and from this had come a fascination in the study of all things aquatic.

Alas, this innocent people had fallen into the trap of allowing their quest for knowledge and discovery to over-ride their natural sense of justice and obligation to those other creatures that shared their perfect world: they fell to the temptation to not only *study* but to *capture* the world of fish and thus developed aquaria in ever greater size and complexity, ostensibly to understand and protect those who shared their watered world, but as time grew to also demonstrate their growing opulence and standing within their own society.

For many centuries, fishing fleets grew across the planet to feed the hunger for the strange, the exotic, the rare, the dangerous, and the most colourful of creatures from their seas. The art of those who fished the depths was to capture without harm any and all fish that they might encounter, to live in mock oceans of peace and tranquillity on display in the homes and mansions of every noble, to form part of the public sea aquaria in every library and university, and to be re-homed in the artificial seas built in the centre of every city.

No hook or net was used but rather the fishermen and fisherwoman would dive into the seas to take by hand with careful concern the fish, flocking to their gentle play. The fish did not fear the fleets: indeed they would glide and toss to catch the shadow of the frail vessels above them as the ships danced full-sailed before the winds, in welcome of the company of those who would dive from the top-sides and mizzen masts in quest of them. But it was many centuries before some dared to ask if the captivity in Mnesis' aquaria was the future that fish-kind would have sought if given a choice?

Shaa'shesh remembered the sudden end of the fish trade and the closure of the aquaria with mixed feelings and deep-felt remorse. Her family had tamed the very seas on which she now looked down; but she alone of many generations of her people had been the first to turn her back on the sea, and she now felt very alone for so doing.

All had changed when one day, she had heard the Founder of her discipleship speak, and her heart and soul had been awoken to the inherent wrong in capturing those that her people loved. In her mind's eye, she cast herself back to that moment of conversion, when as a young child she had first met the Founder, and she contemplated briefly on all it had led to since:

She was five at the time of *The Meeting*, and her parents had still been alive. For her, this was a time of honest happiness, a pause before the plunge, calm before the tempest. One dawn, she had been sitting on the sands of the bay below, waiting for her brothers and father to return from their latest maritime exploration, when a young man had drifted across the strands towards her.

She recalled his eyes, which had been that rarest for her people of clear sapphire blue like her own, so deep and so true. To this day, when she looked into the sky and saw the blue planet of Earth that represented her people's future, she would remember the innocent and compelling eyes of the stranger on the sands. Indeed, as she grew older, she would fall in love several times with other men with those self same rare blue eyes, much to the detriment of her own self esteem and equilibrium, but such was the vulnerability of her open heart.

The stranger's words however had overwhelmed her:

"One day, you will save our people. But first you must save our spirit."

She had stammered out her request for enlightenment, somehow finding the courage to question his words, yet nearly petrified with fear at her comprehension of his revelation and the duty it placed upon her young shoulders. She distrusted the responsibility he described, rather than its source; she considered she was in error as to the meaning of his words or that they were misdirected; that she was being mistaken for another, perhaps? The man's next words left her in no doubt:

"You are Shaa'shesh, daughter of the fisherman, Hera'pel. Your future is written in the stars. Follow me and I will show you *the Path*."

"Where do we go, my Master?" she had replied in all humility.

"We travel to no place but this. Yet I must take your thoughts on a journey through our conversation. Will you follow me?"

"I will gladly listen to you, my Master. I am not afraid to learn new things."

"Do not be afraid," he had replied. "For our world is to come to an end as must all worlds. I am seeking those who will aid me in preparing for that end ... and for a future beyond all ending."

Shaa'shesh had shivered at his words, then as the full import of the end that he foretold struck her, she had pulled away from his hypnotic eyes and run crying towards the maelstrom of the sea, to seek her father and brothers: to somehow draw them from the fury of the waves to the safe haven of the sands. Her fears were all for them, in such danger in their flimsy wooden schooner, vulnerable to the imponderability of the depths, at risk of a solitary end and watery grave amidst Neptune's unfathomable domain.

"They are safe!" the Founder had said and his hand had held her shoulder in reassurance. "Your task however is a hard one. You must help me heal a harm that eats at the soul of our people."

"If my family are safe, then I am your servant in whatever you ask," she had replied from relief at his words of reassurance but also out of curiosity to hear what it was that this man could possibly conceive she could do to aid him.

"I am the Founder not the Master" he had replied. "I am the beginning of something that will save our people from the destruction our world faces and am looking for followers. The Master will come in time to complete the mission of granting our people a future but we have a task we must complete before his arrival."

"Why choose me?"

"Are you willing to help?"

Shaa'shesh had paused for only a split second and then her inherent delight in adventure and her absolute belief in the honesty of those eyes had taken over. She had replied without hesitation:

"Yes."

"Then that is why you have been chosen."

As she had grown older, she had often wondered if she had been mistaken to have agreed so readily to the Founder's request. Indeed, she had not seen the Founder since that day on the crimson sands. It had taken her flight from her foster parents at the age of twelve, and her subsequent meeting with the Master in the capital of *Paraclemos,* to reinforce her belief in the course of action the Founder had set in train. Until that point, all had been in question ... and even now, whenever she headed in retreat to the solace of the *Turbulent Turbot*, she still had regrets, but no longer any doubts.

The task she had been given was simply stated and readily explained, yet looked insurmountable to a young girl of five. As the Founder sat alongside her and offered his insight, she had seen the dilemma she faced and self-doubt had begun to gnaw at her earlier youthful yet naif confidence.

"The end this planet faces will soon be announced by our leading scientists. To meet this pass, this final moment of our perfect world, a leader will one day be elected from amongst the many thousands of our academics in order to find a way that we might survive. This all lies some years ahead of us now, yet it will happen as I describe.

"Our elected leader must have disciples, those who will support him in the difficult days ahead, sometimes even needing to provide him with the courage to go on, or to make the personal sacrifices that he cannot make himself. When you grow up, you will become one of the disciples of our leader, and it is this man, not I, whom you shall call the *Master*. Those you befriend will also become his disciples and thus, when his ministry begins, the Master will have a group of followers he can rely on for their aid, support and absolute loyalty.

"But before this can happen, you must prepare the way for the Master.

"Our people must face the imminence of their destruction with courage *and with purity of heart and spirit.* Alas, we are failing to achieve that purity in one significant regard: despite the wisdom of turning our backs on the death of any living thing created, we still remove the fish of the sea from their native homes and thus disturb the natural order we have been asked to both steward and to hold in reverence. Our continued pursuit of the study of the fish of this world *in captivity* rather than in their own domicile eats at our psyche and our souls.

This is a wrong that we must cease if we are to face our own deaths with a clear conscience.

"Your father commands the largest fleet in this world and is respected amongst all who face the challenge of the seas. If you can persuade him to speak out against the trade that is his livelihood and from which he derives much honour, then there is hope that others will follow suit, and thus we bring to a finish the fashion in aquaria that fuels this foul forage for fish."

"You want me to tell my father to stop fishing?" asked Shaa'shesh and then had gulped at the enormity of the request.

"Yes."

"He will discipline me for my insolence and ignore me. I am only five!"

"Perhaps, but be brave and try. You alone can achieve this," and then the man had stood up and walked slowly into the whirling columns of sand between the two green stone cliff faces that marked the land entrance to the haven from which her father's fleet had set sail. In moments he was a shadow before the storm, then a gap in the circling of the sand, then a pause in time between presence and absence, and finally a distant memory of fate and purpose.

Hera'pel had not beaten Shaa'shesh as she had feared, but he had berated her and sent her to her room in solitude - disciplined through missing the story-telling that evening whilst the rest of her family sat in awe around the open fires on the beaches to listen to the latest adventures of the newly returned fleet.

Shaa'shesh had lain alone that night, her tears of loss mingling with the combined frustration and sorrow of knowing she had failed the Founder.

Yet, as Hera'pel put to sail the following morning, having earlier been greeted by the penitent and loving embrace of his contrite daughter as he had broken his fast, he found that the love of his quest for fish was strangely diminished. Watching the freedom of the sea's inhabitants and reflecting on the tears in Shaa'shesh's eyes, he began for the first time to ponder on the rightness of his endeavours. More than that, he questioned how he had allowed his pursuit of fish to become more important than the love he felt for his daughter, such that he would punish someone he held so precious for merely asking if his trade in sea creatures was right? He admitted to himself he had missed her joyous laughter over the story-telling and thus learnt that most important of lessons: that in punishing those he loved, he had also punished himself.

It had been in reflective mood therefore that he had returned that evening to his family, in order to make the announcement that would change the world of Mnesis, but also come near in time to breaking Shaa'shesh's heart and resolve. His first action had been to run across the sands to lift his daughter high in his arms and then holding her proudly on his shoulders, he had turned to the gathered fleets-men to say:

"I wish you all to know that I love my daughter more than anything else in this world, than my own life, breath, heart and soul. Yesterday, I sought to punish her for asking me if I would stop fishing for her. Today, before you all, I apologise to her and to you that I should have shown such lack of love for she who owns my heart. I am fortunate therefore that despite my error, I have been granted the revelation this day to make amends.

"As I sailed upon the blood-red crests of the shining sea we name the *Revellant*, I looked into its depths and was greeted by the sight of the emperor of all fishes, a giant blue green Turbot of such size and majesty that I knew our family fortune was made. I dove into the sea expecting the Turbot to come to me and looking forwards to the brief play with a fellow creature of the waves, before I would take him carefully as captive for some noble's giant aquaria. Instead the Turbot buffeted me and then headed off into the shallows with me swimming in chase. In time, we surfaced in a large cave, a cutting into the cliffs near to the seaward entrance to our harbour, but previously hidden from our eyes by the combination of a sand bank and tall promontory that stands guard before it.

"My intended catch had taken me to his spawning grounds and before me I saw his family: many thousands of Turbot as proud as he, all swimming amongst the shallows of his grotto in safety from the world of mankind beyond. I surveyed a fortune beyond my wildest dreams. For every aquaria in the land is desperately seeking just one such mighty species of the rare flat fish and before me I had enough to satisfy each and every request.

"I turned, intending to seek the aid of the rest of my crew in bringing this magnificent catch back to land ... to see that many hundreds of the Turbot had gathered as an impenetrable shoal of fish between me and my exit from the cavern. Their teeth were bared in an emotion I had never seen before and hope never to see again. They were offering me the potential of violence if I attempted to leave their home or otherwise seek to give away the whereabouts of their demesne.

"I remember I pleaded with them to release me to no avail, until, in my distress, I finally begged them at least to let me see my daughter again; to offer her the apology I owed her for my poor treatment of her last might. At this, they listened, and as I told them of my argument with Shaa'shesh and its substance, they gathered around me attentively. When I repeated her words to me: "*What we do to fish is not the choice fish would make if we asked them*", then the Turbot had danced in the water before me, before parting to let me go free.

"I can make no promise that what I saw was not some dream from lack of oxygen as I dived too deep, nor the heat of the midday sun burning through reason to make delirium, nor the result of the constant hypnotism of the glittering diamonds that are the moon's reflection on the crest of every wave, but I am mortified that I berated my daughter for her words of wisdom last night. If all else I described is a dream, yet this at least is truth: what we do to the world of fish demeans our souls and our spirits. We avow to treat all creatures with respect and yet we enslave those creatures of the sea for no better wisdom than that it makes us wealthy and is fashionable to display them in our cleverly crafted aquatic cages.

"So, today I make this oath. I shall not seek to capture another fish nor ask any in my fleet to do so. I shall swim with them, play with them and enjoy the miracle that is their beauty in the homes in which they spawn. But I shall not be their captor nor make them my prisoner ever again."

At first, his words had been greeted with scorn and disbelief. It was in mockery of Hera'pel's story that the locals had renamed the pub above the harbour the *Turbulent Turbot*, a fact long forgotten since, except by a daughter who loved her dead father beyond all reason.

Yet, each day thereafter that the fleet took out to sea, at least one captain would return, a startled and stumbling gaze in his eyes, to hang up his sou'wester on its allotted hook above the pub's bar one last time, to shake the hands of Hera'pel who sat patient vigil in the bay window that looked out to the harbour below, his daughter on his knee, holding his arm for comfort. They would mutter a request for forgiveness, pat the head of the pale skinned silent child with the bright blue innocent eyes and purple hair whose words of wisdom they now understood, and then take the long journey to the city in quest for fresh work.

In six months, the fleet was decimated. In a year, the fleet was gone and word had spread to the cities and its institutions of the demise of the fishing trade. It would be wonderful to say that the nobles and academics whom had been the originating source of the trade in fish had the same revelation as those whose lives had been spent in their capture, but, alas, the truth is that fashion changed and when it became difficult to maintain the aquaria, the people of Mnesis looked for something else to show their growing status and wealth. Hera'pel was briefly able to make a living by returning the fish from the abandoned aquaria back to their native homes, but by the time Shaa'shesh was seven, he had neither livelihood nor prospects.

Hera'pel made a visit to his childhood friend Luca on the eastern continent and then on his return, he took ship on a calm sea in his favourite schooner that he had renamed *The Gift of a Daughter,* and was never seen again. The rest of her family blamed Shaa'shesh for his suicide (for surely such a great seas-man as Hera'pel could never have come to grief in the softest of seas save by his own hands?) and indeed, as Shaa'shesh looked back on that saddest of days, she also continued to hold herself to account for her father's death.

Looking out across the bay from the very seat where her father had received the constant surrender of his fleet's captains to the inevitability of the vision of the Founder, her tears of pain and remorse began to flow freely. There was no doubt in her own mind that her father had planned his own end: the choice of his favourite boat and its renaming was just one sad irony perhaps? But the fact that on his visit to Luca he had asked the nobleman to adopt her should he die had provided her with the certainty of her father's terrible intent, when she had found this out some years later.

"May I join you?"

Shaa'shesh sniffed and then looked up mistily from between her golden tears, her mind stumbling into the present from the dark memories of the end she had brought to a childhood of happiness with a loving father. All that had happened since had been a chaotic concussion of tragedy mixed with some remarkable revelations, yet anchored in the crushing knowledge that she had been the cause of death of her own father and, for Shaa'shesh, at least, there could never be inner peace. She looked up into the clear blue sapphire eyes of the stranger from the sands.

"Drink up and then I intend to take you on a boat trip," said the Founder with a grin.

"I cannot swim," replied Shaa'shesh and she gulped.

"M'tew cannot climb trees, but that has not stopped him trying every day since the day you met in our capital! Now cheer up and come with me."

At the news that M'tew was learning to climb trees, Shaa'shesh tears dried up rapidly and she felt a deep glow inside. Her inner-warmth lasted all the way down to the beach, right up to the moment when she saw the name of the Founder's brig: *The Revelation of the Sea.*

"I am to be tested then?" she asked with alarm but all this would elicit was another grin from the Founder and then a raised eyebrow as she hesitated to climb in. "Rats" she muttered to herself and then laughed: "I did choose this after all," she remembered, recalling their first encounter. So sticking her tongue out briefly in the Founder's direction, she skipped into the brig and sat nonchalantly at its stern. He cast off and they headed into the solemnity of the seas where the furthest horizons meet the deepest of dark destinies.

As the sun stood upon the rim of their world, both sky and sea blazed dark purple, and the moon and the stars lit every passing crest as silver strands, so the Founder stood in the prow and the story of her father's end came to life in the shadows around her.

She saw his schooner, its name of remembrance in glittering gold letters carved upon a dark oaken varnished hull, sailing slowly towards the hidden cave where the Turbots held imperial rule over the shadowy shallows of a sunken sandy grotto. Suddenly came the realisation that his intent was not his own death but rather the desire to say goodbye to the Turbots and to prove to himself his vision of them had been real after all - to justify his actions and the financial ruin to which he had brought his family through them. She could listen to his thoughts: his pride still in the wisdom, beauty, loyalty and love of his daughter; his own self pride and self worth in having turned his back on wealth and towards a better purpose; and yet tempered with the remote possibility that it had all been some delusion.

The fish had greeted his coming with great joy. Indeed, such was their delight that they had leapt in their hundreds and thousands upon his decks to meet and greet him: to show him that all he had done had been for real. To remove all of his self doubt. He jumped over the side to play with them in the warm waters of the sea and was mobbed by their pleasure. But then the seas-man in him saw that disaster would strike.

Such were the numbers leaping into his boat that the fish were in danger of becoming stranded and suffocating under their own weight ... yet in their delirium they could not stop themselves questing for the comfort of him who had saved them in ever increasing numbers. He climbed back onto his schooner and tried in desperation to prevent the fish from jumping on board, seeking also to lift them by the armful back into the sea. Yet, he could not do so quickly enough without fear of harming them.

Hera'pel looked down from the top of his pilot house on the largest catch of fish that he or any man in the whole of Mnesis had ever taken and knew what he must do.

He scuttled his ship, knowing that only in this way could he prevent the fish in their frenzy from slaying themselves. As he sank with his vessel, the fish tried to save him, in turn, but the cold seeped into his muscles and stopped his breathing. So, with a sad smile, he passed into the depths, his final thought being that at least he had settled things well for Shaa'shesh.

"Could this not have been prevented?" gasped Shaa'shesh, holding her knees tightly in the pain of what she had seen. The Founder replied sternly:

"The Composer could prevent the end of Mnesis, but then the end of the planet Earth would become certain. The Composer could have saved your father, but then you would not have met Luca, been forced from his household into homelessness and come to *Paraclemos* to meet the Master, just in time, I might add, to give Sala'am the resolve he was lacking to find a way to save our people. Yes, all *could* have been prevented. Yet good has come of this and your father died fulfilled. Be happy at this revelation, my daughter, and know you were not the cause of your father's death but rather the source of his pride."

"Can I see my father again?" the young girl asked.

"Of course" replied the Founder as a new southerly wind caught the sails and a beam swung across the prow from east to west whilst the brig swung north before the force of the gale, casting Shaa'shesh like a puppet into the surrounding waves.

"Remember the Revelation of the Sea" cried the blue eyed man into the roaring of the waters that dragged at Shaa'shesh's skirts and then she sank under the first wave and could neither see nor hear him any longer.

Her skirts were made of heavy brocade and silk. Rapidly filling with water, they dragged her deeper and deeper below the purple surface into the darkness of the depths. She opened her mouth to scream, then to pray, and felt her lungs fill as the water rushed hungrily through mouth and nose. She felt the soaring pain of pressure building up behind her eyes and the growing headache that comes with oxygen deprivation. The muscles around her lungs tightened and then ceased to function under the weight of the water within and without. Stars briefly appeared before her eyes and with it came the image of her father smiling. She heard his whispered benison: "I love you with all my heart" and then she felt the blessed black relief of unconsciousness.

"There is no salvation save through you. There is no salvation save through you. There is no salvation save through you."

Briefly, Shaa'shesh wondered who might be reciting the final words of the *Revelation of the Sea* in such repetitive desperation and then realised that the words were hers. She felt numb. She felt incredibly cold. Yet, she could feel the warming touch of another's hand holding hers, and the welcome comfort of a cloak across her shivering shoulders. She felt she was not yet ready to open her eyes but also that some sign of gratitude was needed for whoever had rescued her from the sea, and so gave the hand a little squeeze. In response, Shaa'shesh heard a half-trembling sob from just above her left shoulder and so decided purely out of curiosity to take a peek. Looking down on her was the tear-stained face of Ptere'an, his right hand grasping her own, as if the whole world depended on it.

"How ...?" she began to ask, and then was hit with a tide of nausea and rolled over quickly to cough up two lungs full of water and a stomach full of lichen. The headache that immediately followed took what little of her breath away at which she groaned ruefully: "To have a headache like this when I have never drunk a drop of alcohol in my life, is, I think, so very unfair!" Ptere'an gave her a hug in relief at the return of his friend.

"It was the fish," he replied to her half answered question. "They carried you to land. I have never seen anything like it in my life. They did so in their thousands, in turns, and I was not alone to see it. Every type of fish imaginable, large and small, those we deem as killers and those who are harmless, all working in concert. They have gone now. Yet many of us watched from the windows of the *Turbulent Turbot* and none can recall a spectacle like this before. I have sent for help as you are cold from being in the water and you were near death from drowning. Help is on its way, I promise you, and we will have you warm and safe soon. But I must ask: what does this all mean? How were you saved in this way?"

"Tell me first why so many are gathered at the *Turbulent Turbot*? For it has not been known for such popularity for many years. Tell me this, and then I have another story for you. One I think that shall go well in the disc that we prepare as the testimony for our world."

"There is no big mystery. I received a stranger's call that you might be in trouble at sea here and so brought with me some of your father's friends from the city. I knew they were familiar with this coastline, so it seemed sensible to ask them to come to your aid. They all admire you for something you once did as a child, but will not tell me what you did. When word got out that you were in trouble, they flocked in their hundreds to return to their old haunting ground and come to your rescue. We flew here in time to see you rise up from the sea on a wave of marine life."

Through the floodgate's opening of her weeping, Shaa'shesh's eyes sparkled as she looked up at Ptere'an and said: "Then I have a story to tell you and anyone else who will hear. *This is a story that will make us all proud*. For the fish saved me because of something my father once did for them. Get me into some warm clothes, give me a roaring fire, and the *Turbulent Turbot*'s best coffee, then nothing, not even the end of the world, is going to stop me telling this story."

Thus it was that the sixth of the twelve accounts to go onto the disc that would be sent in safety to the planetoid of Pallas was **the story of Hera'pel and the huge catch of fish he let go.**

Shaa'shesh wept for days, held close by the companionable silence of Ptere'an and her father's friends as she did so. For those around her knew that her tears were those of healing. And at their gentle cleansing flow, the doom of the approaching asteroid appeared in the minds of the people of Mnesis to recede ever further into the distance.

Chapter Eight: Za'astra

Shaa'shesh stood nervously on the podium at the north east section of the huge amphitheatre in the centre of the *Bibliotechnaoi* and prepared to fulfil a promise she had made rashly to the Master on the first day of his *story feste*.

A small crowd had gathered on hearing that the Master's disciple was to speak and this had only added to her disquiet. She looked up into the skies, and felt some reassurance as she saw the clear ice blue heavens above her, took a deep breath, inhaled the fresh spring air, the taste of the first narcissi on her tongue, the bitter scent of cherry blossoms assailing her nostrils.

Then she grinned: she so loved the taste and aroma of spring. For now her trees would be at their most splendid. With the image of the gift of their many hues vibrant in her mind, new courage came to her from the knowledge that whatever reaction her telling might receive, there were greater things in this world to return to.

The amphitheatre of *Paraclemos* was a complete circle of banked and terraced stone seating, looking down upon six revolving stages, each with its own podium and audio-visual display screen. It had been so designed to enable multiple simultaneous performances, and thus to encourage the people of Mnesis to sample the many different styles of the performing arts, replicating the continuous street theatre outside, where conjurers would collide with classical composers and play-writers competed with poets in a cacophony of comedy and tragedy, art and theatre, music and dance.

Some of the crowd that had gathered had chosen to hire silk cushions and sit high above the young disciple. The acoustics of the amphitheatre were so perfect that they would capture her every whispered breath, no matter where they sat, whilst from their top-perch on the highest banks of seating, they could look across to the green waters of the *Falls of Laiden*, or spread themselves out on blankets and enjoy a picnic, even lie back and sleep, should the performance below become too wearisome.

The rest of the crowd stood on the sanded floor of the theatre immediately before Shaa'shesh, ready to heckle politely should her performance fail or falter, or worse to walk away and desert her, should they become bored. Shaking with fear, the girl began softly, so quietly that the crowd had to lean forward to hear her:

"I have no story of heroism to tell upon this day,
Nor a happy ending to send you on your way
... with heartsease and souls aglow.

I offer no wisdom to test the synapses of your minds.
Or some new philosophy to strengthen the values of this land
I bear no gift of laughter or the words to make my tale kind:
My characters are forgettable, their actions shadows in lost time.
I offer no bridge to fulfilment or an uncovered testimony to love
No road to new discovery or pathway to HE who dwells above

Enlightenment through entertainment stretches my skill beyond its limit
A symphony of words is a composition for which I am sadly unfit
I cannot hope to command attention with my uncomplicated account

But ask in humility you look beyond the inadequacy of my talent

To see the simplicity in my story of a brave young family
whose love for their surroundings forged this mighty plea:

All shall be as happy as we, despite our encroaching end;
the choice is ours: to make our peace, our broken pasts to mend
In this city that we herald as the princely Paraclemos
many seek their fortunes, as many find pain and loss.

Too oft we confuse the wealth of status for an answer to our fears
Miss the beauty of God's creation through eyes filled with bitter tears!"

At which, choked with the first of many tears, golden streaks upon the rose-like glow of her cheeks, she fell silent, not sure if she could find the courage to continue.

"Tell us!" the crowd answered in surprised awe. "Have heart! Have courage! Hold nothing back!" and even those on the highest terraces stood to hear the whispered words of the disciple, whilst those at Shaa'shesh's feet gathered closer to touch her; to hold her firm to the stage lest she run away in her obvious terror at the ordeal of her story-telling; to be assured she was not the fickle wind, so delicate was her quiet and stumbling voice, so inadequate her command upon the podium.

"There lives in our city, a young family. A man, honourable and proud, who once made a single mistake, instantly forgiven, but who now bears the greatest of burdens in recompense. His wife is serenely beautiful and totally loyal. Yet she is saddened that in these final days of our planet, she must sacrifice her most precious thing: time with her husband, for the sake of his new responsibilities. They have a daughter, named Za'astra, who is profoundly unwell, yet a beacon of happiness for any who visit their humble household *with an open-mind*.

One day, they were visited by a young disciple, sent by the Master. For it had been heard that Za'astra was unwell, and the Master believed she might benefit from the healing presence of one of his Chosen.

Alas, the disciple he sent was inadequate to the task: she was damaged from before that time and unable to see fully the force of familial love in those she met. She saw only sickness where there was also health.

The disciple was full of self-doubt and self-despite, erroneously believing she had been the cause of her own father's death many years earlier. The disciple had no inner peace upon which to draw. Outwardly, she offered calm assurance, but within she was deeply disturbed.

When the disciple reached the home of the young family, she had been both surprised at and welcoming of its lack of ostentation. From a humble background herself and having spent many years amongst the homeless in our city, the young girl warmed to the utilitarianism of her surroundings. No item of furniture save that needed for the essential purposes of life: no display cabinets; no dressers; no side tables; no ornaments; no pictures, wall-hangings or paintings; simply racks upon racks of books, a much-loved and weathered sofa, a table and two benches, an oven and sink, and a wet room beyond. A single stone staircase then led to the two bed chambers above, and it was to the smaller of the two rooms, that the disciple was guided by worried parents in order to meet Za'astra.

Za'astra was sitting on her bed facing the single window of her room, looking out across a small balcony towards the myriad of rooftop gardens of her neighbours. Her view was breathtaking. It was as if all of nature had woken to greet the child in an embrace of scent and colour, shape and hue. Herbs, flowers and blossoms of every species paid homage to her thoughtful and appreciative gaze, vying for her solemn attention. She gazed out in awe and wonder as the sun shone through her frail flesh, rendering her fragility translucent to the disciple's eyes.

Her father saw a shining angel bathed in the light of creation; the disciple saw a sick child in need of rapid hospitalisation and spoke for the first time since entering their home:

"Your daughter needs help. I will take her with me."

The emotion unleashed by her words was a new thing to our world. The father experienced a unique feeling called *anger* and, to protect his daughter from the threat of removal from the view from her bedroom window that she so loved, he rained blows down on the bewildered disciple, forcing her from his house to collapse under the weight of his violence upon the street outside. He might have slain the young disciple in his ire, had not Za'astra run down and stood between them:

"Hear my prayer!" the dying girl had said simply yet steadfastly. And the father's anger had fled instantly before her tranquil plea:

"In friendship and love we can meet every challenge."

As Shaa'shesh remembered that moment, suddenly she found she could not continue her story-telling. Her remorse at her insensitivity on that day over a year ago now, her new-found revelation that she had not after all been the cause of her father's death, her recent reconciliation with M'tew, the man she loved, all overwhelmed her. Above all, her heart ached for the friendship she had found with Ptere'an, a companionship born out of that simple prayer of Za'astra. She stood silenced, never having felt more alone, shaking with shame, grief and the final realisation of her public humiliation.

Ptere'an had been in his office watching his monitors for the stories of that day when he had seen Shaa'shesh approach the podium. He had been surprised at how nervous she was; no sign of her usual ebullience and self-confidence. Then he had listened to the start of her tale and within seconds had hit his intercom to command his official transporter to be made ready: "To the *Bibliotechnaoi* and make haste!" he had cried "or my daughter will never forgive me."

Shaa'shesh was blinded by her own tears, so never saw Ptere'an arrive, running through the astonished and bewildered crowd, to leap up onto the podium and hold his friend in the tightest of embraces. Her first knowledge of him was his strong arms around her, at which she let her head fall onto his chest in sorrow and dismay. This time it was Ptere'an who took charge and provided the strength they both needed to go on. Standing tall, but never for a moment letting go of his grip on the girl at his side who clung to him as to the rock after which he was named, he turned to those assembled in the amphitheatre, and to the recorders that would broadcast his words to the many thousands that had tuned in to hear the penitence and confession of the Master's favourite disciple, then without fear or hesitation, spoke calmly for them all to hear:

"Shaa'shesh is to return to my house where it is the wish of my wife, my daughter and myself that she offers the power of her healing to my daughter, Za'astra. For Shaa'shesh has done no wrong in our eyes. It is only in the grief of her own heart that she believes she has erred; no-one else thinks this of her. She asks too much of herself and forgets she is a true friend, full of love ... and loved by us all in return."

"Yes Shaa'shesh is loved by us all" whispered the crowd, nodding at first and then their acknowledgement of this fact grew louder and louder. Yet still Shaa'shesh's head hung in shame, until one young man, standing at the very furthest wing of the amphitheatre, shouted above the noise of the crowd:

"**Shame on you Shaa'shesh**. Have you already forgotten the prayer of Za'astra? In our friendship and love, you can meet this challenge."

"Oh!" exclaimed the young disciple, as the moment of revelation finally came. "It really is that simple, isn't it?" and she looked up laughing into Ptere'an's twinkling eyes, as he whispered joyfully:

"Welcome back!"

Later that evening, Shaa'shesh stooped to give Za'astra the sign of peace. She remained very concerned at the fever that seemed to have gripped the frail young child without surcease. Despite her best intent and endeavours, the disciple still had no answer to the illness she saw before her, but she knew better now than to voice her inner fears or to offer to remove the girl from her contemplation of the beauty of creation.

Soft tears of sorrowing sadness fell slowly as the first drops of spring rained upon Shaa'shesh's cheeks to tumble gently onto Za'astra's pale yet shining face. Bending forwards to kiss those tears away, the two girl's lips touched ... **and a sequence of events was set in train that would one day see the miracle of sentient life begin on a distant blue planet named Earth**.

There were few on Mnesis who believed in the power of prayer. Faith in a supreme being was a rare thing to find amongst the peaceful and wise people of this doomed world, and Shaa'shesh's privately held beliefs in a divine will were an exception rather than the rule.

Yet such was the tolerance of this society for any and all words of beauty, that Za'astra's simple prayer was repeated in the bars and cafes, shops and libraries, offices and homes, courtyards and corridors, whenever and wherever the people of Mnesis needed the comfort and solace to know that they were not alone with their fears.

Thus it was that the seventh story to be included on the disc that would one day be sent to the safety of the planetoid Pallas, as a testimony to the people of Mnesis, **was the short prayer of a young girl**, dying slowly from a strange disease, yet whose thoughts were never for herself but rather for all that she saw and loved as she looked out from the small casement window of her bedroom.

At each repetition of Za'astra's innocent plea, the doom of the approaching asteroid appeared in the minds of the people of Mnesis to recede ever further into the distance.

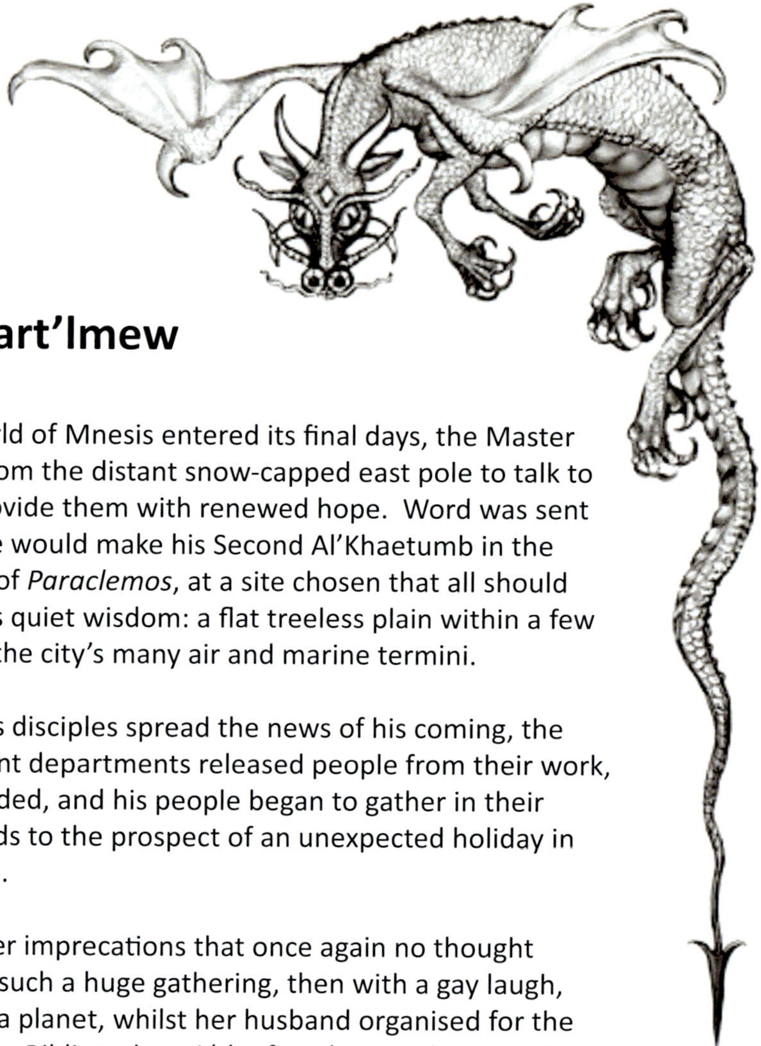

Chapter Nine: Bart'lmew

As the peaceful world of Mnesis entered its final days, the Master returned briefly from the distant snow-capped east pole to talk to his people and provide them with renewed hope. Word was sent out across the land that he would make his Second Al'Khaetumb in the desert plains to the north of *Paraclemos*, at a site chosen that all should be able to see and hear his quiet wisdom: a flat treeless plain within a few hours walking distance of the city's many air and marine termini.

His summons went out, his disciples spread the news of his coming, the Academies and Government departments released people from their work, the *story feste* was suspended, and his people began to gather in their thousands, looking forwards to the prospect of an unexpected holiday in the warmth of a bright sun.

Numa'mesh muttered bitter imprecations that once again no thought had been given to feeding such a huge gathering, then with a gay laugh, prepared enough food for a planet, whilst her husband organised for the *College of Academiae* at the *Bibliotechnaoi* (the five thousand Lectors from whom the Master had been elected five years earlier) to collect and ferry the food to the meeting place selected by Sala'am.

Shaa'shesh moaned at the absence of any trees near the site, so used her "authority" as Ptere'an's assistant to requisition one of her planet's orbiting research geo-satellites to undertake a quick tree survey. To her relief and delight, she discovered a lonely copse of six tall, proud Cyprus trees about a mile from the place of summonsing and headed off to reserve her perch in the companionable comfort of their branches.

As'tol was the *Guildmaster of the Tentmakers*, whose Temple of silks and canvas sat proudly in the marbled Curia, their gaily coloured awnings and tentings facing the more classical Doric columns and carved oak-panelled doors that gave entrance to the *Bibliotechnaoi*, at the heart of *Paraclemos*. His Guild had been the first to recognise the importance of literature for the people of Mnesis. The nomads of the deserts had spread the *Gift of Telling* across all lands and time, always holding the bard, poet and play-write in reverence and awe. Thus, his Guild had located itself, many centuries earlier, in pride of place opposite the grand entrance to the great library that was his planet's most important achievement.

On reading the news of the Master's summons, and on seeing the huge convoys of food being sent out into the desert, As'tol issued instruction for tents of all sizes and shapes to be made ready to provide covering for the food, shelter for the vulnerable in the heat, privacy for those who would seek to bathe, discretion for those who sought comfort in the intimacy of another. "We shall create a caravanade of such size and hue and fantastical delight that it shall seem as if a mobile city of silk has arrived in the desert, to disappear as magically with the first crimson delight of the following dawn!" His Guild members nodded in silent glee, enthused by his vision, and then set to work. But no-one replied to the wise man's words ... for all knew that As'tol was deaf.

As'tol's closest friend was an old man named Bart'lmew. They would drink iced tea in quiet companionship, working their way around the souks of the city, choosing a different location each day for some wonderful new sight, or for the sound of the crowds, or birdsong, or a solitary marbled fountain, their own silence occasionally broken by As'tol's detailed and precise descriptions of their surroundings.

For Bart'lmew was blind and relied on As'tol's eyes to comprehend the wonders of the world in which they moved.

He had no regrets over his loss of sight which had crept up on him slowly as he had aged; he still had many memories of a time with sight and in particular of the stories he had once read as an honoured Lector and lecturer in literature. He did regret he could not repay As'tol's generosity by becoming his friend's ears, in the way that As'tol had become Bart'lmew's sight.

As the huge crowd gathered on the *Flats of the Calming Crail,* As'tol stole away from the chaos of the erection of the many marquees and desert barques, to find his friend and guide him to a quiet and peaceful spot from which he might hear the new guidance of the Master. A mile to the north of where the food hall had just gone up, to the mighty cheers of those waiting expectantly outside to sample

Numa'mesh's latest culinary marvels and creations, As'tol had spotted a small clump of trees: an ideal location for Bart'lmew to sit in the shade yet hear the Master's oratory at work.

As'tol himself would welcome being at some distance from the rest of his Guild as they erected their great tents. He had sadly realised long ago that they found him *in the way*, unable as he was to respond to their shouted instructions and commands to each other. Yet they were too kind and reverent of his standing amongst them to ever have said or implied this. Nonetheless, As'tol knew they would get on quicker and better without him, and he would enjoy the day more in the company of a friend who looked beyond his disability to his underlying generous nature.

The two friends reached the isolated copse of Cyprus trees, a flask of their favourite iced tea with sherbet in a rucksack on Bart'lmew's back, and as they went to sit down, the discussion that is the subject of our eighth story began with the blind-man indicating that he would like to climb the tree in order to hear the Master better (or so As'tol interpreted his companion's frenetic combination of mime, mouthed sentences and waving arms).

"You want to go up a tree?"

Bart'lmew nodded vigorously.

"You crazy old man. You will fall down. And I cannot climb up after you to get you, so do not go far!"

Nonetheless, As'tol did not hesitate but hoisted the old man onto his shoulders and then guided his arms such that they could clasp the lowest of the branches to haul himself up. Fate, or something else, determined that As'tol should choose one particular tree out of the six before him. Even on the last day, As'tol could not explain why he chose the tree he did, but he was to be glad he did so.

Bart'lmew sat on a firm branch and let his legs swing out to the sides and then in front of him, embracing the freedom of being above the ground whilst listening to the sound of the large crowds massing before the Master. As Bart'lmew's legs stretched out along the branch, from below As'tol saw something move amongst the leaves and called out to his friend, but Bart'lmew was too engrossed in the sound of the multitude to hear:

"Bart'lmew, look out!"

The old man's added weight on the branch caused the end to vibrate manically until it snapped with a loud crack, detaching itself from the rest of the tree and falling to the ground, depositing with it the girl who had been lying asleep in its furthest reaches. She hit the ground with a thud, woke up, and exclaimed with her customary acceptance of such unplanned yet frequent hard landings: "Ouch!"

"Are you hurt?" asked a concerned Bart'lmew from above her head, whilst As'tol stooped down to help the girl rise.

"Only my pride, honoured sirs" the girl replied, but tested her limbs carefully just to make sure and then grinned when all seemed to be working as her God had intended, though a little more delicately than usual. Bart'lmew was still contrite however and insisted on dismounting from the tree that he might check the girl was free from injury for himself. So As'tol and their newly made companion, the fallen dryad, helped the old man back to the ground. The blind-man's first action was to carefully inspect every joint with his gentle hands to ensure she was really free from trauma, and only when he was satisfied, did he relax into a smile and then began to chuckle:

"Asleep up a tree when meant to be listening to the Master! There is only one person in the whole of Mnesis who would do such a thing, surely? You are Shaa'shesh and I am pleased at last to meet you."

She bowed to As'tol, whom she recognised from his Guildmaster's robes, and then took Bartl'mew's hand and raised it to her own lips in acknowledgement:

"Yes, I am Shaa'shesh. I am at your service, honoured sirs," then pointed to her disciple's robes for the benefit of As'tol that he might understand the meaning of her conversation with Bart'lmew.

"What good your hearing you crazy man?" laughed As'tol "When you cannot hear this disciple snoring!"

"What good your sight, you old rascal?" Bart'lmew replied, chuckling himself. "It was you put me up the same tree as this poor girl. Lucky she came to no harm!"

Then both turned towards each other and the same thought came into their heads. Bart'lmew nodded and As'tol said: "Yes" at which the older man turned back to the disciple:

“Forgive us, my newly found friend, but it seems that As’tol and I are in agreement that your advice would be most welcome on something that has taxed us for years. Would you be willing to answer one question?”

Again, Shaa’shesh bowed to As’tol then took Bart’lmew’s hand as acknowledgement of her acceptance, saying as she did so:

“I promise to make answer. I can make no promise that my answer will make sense or be sensible. But I am not known to be silent on any matter - indeed my many friends doubt I can be silent *at all* unless sleeping.”

Bart’lmew beckoned towards As’tol, giving his friend permission to ask the disciple the question on which they had pondered over many cups of tea:

“If you could choose to keep one of the senses, which would it be?”

Shaa’shesh’s initial reaction was to laugh. But then she realised that for these men, pride in their abilities and independence using their remaining senses was intermingled with a deep yet bravely disguised sense of loss for the one sense on which each could no longer rely. She chose therefore another path - to turn the laughter on herself but also to reflect the question back to the questioners. To Bart’lmew she said:

“The senses I *still possess* will always be the most important but no sense comes without its risks. You know the phrase: speak, hear, see no wrong, or wrong becomes your world?”

For the benefit of As’tol, she took a stick and drew three faces. One with the ears covered (below which she drew the letter A), one with eyes covered (below which she drew the letter B) and then one with mouth covered (the implication being obvious that this was Shaa’shesh herself).

The two men paused. And then the ridiculousness of the suggestion that Shaa’shesh could live without the ability to speak gripped all three of them simultaneous and they laughed until their eyes streamed with tears and their ribs ached.

“Nice try! As’tol finally gasped. “But for such a totally inadequate answer, it is in my mind that we should put you to the test, young disciple!” at which Bart’lmew nodded his agreement and continued his friend’s thought: “One day with your ears covered such that you cannot hear and one day blindfolded such that you cannot see. Answer our question in two day's time and we hope you shall be wiser for your experience."

As these words were spoken, the Master concluded his Address before the multitude and then returned to his transporter that was waiting in the sands behind him to take him back to the Space Port at Melchor. But not before he had looked across the Flats to where Shaa'shesh stood dumb-founded at the challenge she now faced. The Master's parting words seemed, in this rare moment of her having finally been silenced, to be aimed deliberately at her:

"In the little time remaining, I ask you to have the courage to explore new things; to see our world through the eyes of others; to hear our world in the words of others; to hold what you have left very dear; and never to bend to the fear of a doom that we can make have a meaning beyond all hope. Let us not think of what we have lost or will lose in the coming months, but rather of what we have done and will achieve. This will survive us all as a precious memory for a child-like cosmos which is still developing; a universe that needs an example of faith to follow in the billions of years ahead."

"I accept" said the poor girl, feeling that she had been completely and utterly set up by the Master, the Guildmaster and his blind friend.

Two days later, As'tol and Bart'lmew sat down at a chrome table beneath a striped parasol on the lime stone terrace of a shaded souk that overlooked the ancient quayside of *Paraclemos.* One could see and the other could hear the gentle lapping of the bright yellow water, the constant creaking movement of the shallow gondolas emblazoned in reds and gold and greens, the boisterous chatter and challenging benign mockery of the gondolieri, waiting to offer their fares to strangers seeking a unique tour of the city's history and mythology. The most fantastical stories on the planet were told upon these fragile barges which had graced the clear waterways of this citadel for as long as the people of Mnesis could remember.

"Iced sherbet," they asked in unison of the waiter before ever he could request their order. At which he smiled, recognising them as regulars, and within moments the brass pitcher and crystal glasses, porcelain bowl of iced rose water, broken sugar canes, a small iron pestle and mortar, and cedar box of crushed lemon sherbet, chillies and ginger arrived at their table.

"Relaxing or blow your head off?" enquired As'tol. Bart'lmew mimed going to sleep to indicate he would rather relax. As'tol mixed him his drink, avoiding the chillies and ginger, then passed the sherbet across the table and guided his hand to show where the glass could be found. Bart'lmew nodded in gratitude and sipped his drink, enjoying both the aroma and its refreshing sharpness. Some devilry in As'tol, on the other hand, determined him to go for adventure and so he mixed in some ginger and added a crushed chilli to the sherbet and sugar in the mortar before transferring the mix to his own glass. Then with a devil may care smile, he gulped down his first sip. Bart'lmew could only laugh as moments later he heard the waiter rush across the terrace to pat As'tol on the back - his face had turned bright purple; his eyes burning red.

When finally As'tol recovered his breath, and his taste buds, he joined in the laughter before asking his friend: "Is it not today we hear from our young and foolish disciple?"

"It is!" acknowledged Bart'lmew, nodding for his friends benefit but then muttering to himself, "Though I think we were unfair on her."

As'tol shook his head to indicate he had not understood the second part of what Bart'lmew had said, but the blind-man did not see, and for a brief moment both men shared a sadness that even after all these years, communication between them remained limited. "We asked the girl the wrong question," they both admitted in unison. "We should have asked for her help that we can understand each other better! We missed our opportunity I fear."

The silence that followed their revelation was disturbed by the sound of someone running. Bart'lmew heard the urgency of someone panting and out of breath, and turned his head to capture more. But it was Ast'ol who picked out the sight of a young carer, a seeker in clear distress, hurrying between the tables along the quayside in questing anxiety. She stopped to talk to the waiter briefly who pointed towards the two men. As'tol was curious but not yet alarmed; Bart'lmew, however, with his acute hearing, had clearly overheard the request made of the waiter and turned to his friend in concern:

"It is not good news, I am afraid" but once again As'tol was unable to decipher his words.

The carer reached their table and without hesitation, blurted out her tragic news:

"Come, come quickly! Shaa'shesh fell badly. She is so severely injured we fear she is dying. She calls for you, Bart'lmew."

"Fetch the waiter's laptop so that you can type this news for my friend to read. He will worry unless he knows where I go" the blind-man asked. "Then take me to the girl. This is my doing and I will atone."

Bart'lmew was driven to the City Infirmary in an air transporter summoned by the waiter and with the worried carer as his escort. She was able to tell him very little, save that Shaa'shesh had fallen from one of the tallest fir trees in the city and broken several bones in her fall, before being found unconscious at the foot of the tree. Even now, she was feared to have sustained multiple brain injuries, as, in her delirium, she had referred to having been without hearing or was it sight over the last two days. The injured girl's confusion was such that she seemed to think she had lost both at some time or another, yet there was no sign of any impairment?

"We cannot make any sense out of her. She says she climbed a tree blindfold. Her brain injuries must be severe. For who in their right mind would do such a thing, let alone think they had?"

"Oh!" exclaimed Bart'lmew and tried not to chuckle as he began to realise what had happened. Then he continued: "Does she make sense in all other regards?"

"Not really. She keeps saying she has the answer to the question you did not ask and that is why she must see you. We all fear she must be dying."

By the time, Bart'lmew had arrived at the Infirmary, Ptere'an was there to greet him at the entrance-way with more encouraging news. "Bang to the head, broken elbow, broken wrist, two cracked ribs, sprained ankle, bruised coccyx, damaged pride, black eye, nasty cut on thigh that has been stitched, likely to be in bed for maybe a day, knowing her, before she tries to climb another tree, but otherwise she is fine. If she is talking nonsense then that is normal too," he added for the benefit of the anxious carer. "And she definitely wants to see you, Bart'lmew. I will take you up."

Bart'lmew stepped nervously into the room, guided by Ptere'an. But before either man could approach the bed where Shaa'shesh lay fiddling in her boredom with the various bits of equipment and wiring that plugged into the bedside monitors, she looked up, and then hopped on her good leg into Bart'lmew's arms to give the old man a reassuring hug.

"I want you to know I am alright," she said in a rush, "and that it was wrong for people to worry you about me."

Unwittingly, she had pulled the leads out of the monitoring devices above her bed, and alarms went off both inside the room and at the monitoring station by the Carers' station. Carers rushed from all directions as the cardiac crash alarm was set off: "Cardiac Team to room 12. Cardiac Team to room 12. Heart event indicated. Heart event indicated."

Somewhat sheepishly, Shaa'shesh obeyed their orders for her to return back to bed.

"If she moves again, hit her over the head with these," muttered one of the carers to Ptere'an, handing him the crutches they had tried to persuade the girl to use earlier, and which Shaa'shesh had flung under her bed in disgust at being treated as an invalid. "Worst patient we have ever had," another added and all of the carers had nodded in agreement before filing out of the room to leave the two men alone with the unrepentant girl. As soon as the door closed on them, Shaa'shesh stuck her tongue out at their departing backs, before turning with a brilliant smile towards Ptere'an:

"Could you leave us too? I need to talk to Bart'lmew for a few moments."

"You behave," he admonished her then left them alone.

"Hold my hand," she asked the old man. "Come towards my voice, there is nothing in your way and my hand is being held out towards your right hand." Bart'lmew did as she asked and she grasped his right hand carefully, before turning it palm upwards. "This is the shape of the letter A" and she traced a symbol in his hand as she had in the sand on the day they had met, "and this is the letter B."

Suddenly, revelation came to Bart'lmew:

"I can trace letters in the palm of As'tol's hands, just as you did in the sand, and he will understand me?" he asked querulously.

"I will teach both As'tol and you to trace the letters and to understand them. I have also devised symbols for our five hundred most common words and you can work out many more between yourselves. You are both clever and will grasp this new language quickly. It is my gift to you both for the revelation you have given me in return."

"So you have answered our challenge?"

"Yes. I went up my tree when deaf and could not hear the birds. So I went up my tree when blind and fell."

"I do not understand," replied the old man. "What is the wisdom you learnt from this?"

"That neither hearing nor sight is the most important sense. The answer to your question is that the most important sense is the sense of pain. It is the pain I feel now that will ensure I never fall for one of your challenges again!"

Bart'lmew's laughter was so loud that even his friend As'tol heard it on this one occasion, as he sat waiting nervously by the quayside for the return of his blind comrade, little knowing the new dawn to which their long friendship had just awoken.

Thus it was that the eighth story to be included on the disc that would one day be sent to the safety of the planetoid Pallas, as a testimony to the people of Mnesis, **was the story of a blind man who learnt to bridge the divide between his loss of sight and his friend's loss of hearing**.

As each day, As'tol and Bart'lmew grew more proficient in the sign language they continued to develop, their newfound communion carried them throughout the public places of the city. At the sight of their joy in each other's company, the doom of the approaching asteroid appeared in the minds of the people of Mnesis to recede ever further into the distance.

Chapter Ten: Perditus

It was the talk of every bar and grove. All were in agreement. Never had the planet Mnesis looked so glorious or been so hypnotically fascinating than in those days of their final summer. It was as if nature understood the end that was approaching and had decided to make one last great demonstration of its indescribable beauty in gratitude to and in solace for a people who had taken on their duty to steward this world with diligence, reverence and care.

The approaching asteroid played its part as its gravity made subtle alterations to the once steady and predictable progression of this idyll's seasons. The first signs of change were the water spouts that began to drift across The Revellant, blue and green towers of crystallised water gliding imperiously over the flat crimson seas. They were greeted with awe and delight, sparking new stories of marine deity for the story feste that now progressed through day and night.

Belepheron erupted for the first time in centuries. An event their seismographs had happily predicted in time for all to be at a suitable distance. Orama and Eli'shah sat happily upon a small skiff to watch the firework display as the giant mountain deluged their former excavation at the neighbouring *Mount Becilaph* with diamonds. She already had her diamond, placed on her ring finger firmly and with love only a few days earlier, before an assembled gathering of their fellow students, by the fun-loving man to whom she had pledged the rest of her life.

The seas rose slightly bringing back to life the dry rivers of the deserts, whilst the land winds slept to reveal clear blue daytime skies. In a rush, the flowers of the sands grasped their opportunity to erupt before the sun. At night, the stars shone silver amidst swirling purple, green and red nebulae created by the dust trail left in the wake of the asteroid.

Spontaneous showers of warm water would refresh those caught within the torch-like heat of the midday sun, whilst the twilight tossing seas came crashing against the quaysides, to douse the many eager watchers in their fine dew-like spray.

The blossoms of spring never departed, the narcissi held their ground, tulips continued to grow amidst the blue grass lawns, but to their colour and majesty were added the bouquet and hues of the summer bloom: the scent of roses and blackcurrant, the ripeness of apple and pear, lavender and lilac, lemons and limes, strawberries and sage, corn and thyme, daisies and delphiniums, damsons and grapevines. There was no frost to damage the magnolias nor heavy rain to flatten the poppy heads as all flowers and fruit rose out of their true time.

Sitting halfway up the *Hill of Charmant,* in a secluded spot beneath the welcome shade of a mallorn tree, Shaa'shesh looked down on the *Plains of Relish* and towards her home city of *Paraclemos*. She had never seen the plains look so stunningly beautiful before in her life and whispered "Thank you thank you thank you!" over and over again to herself. Had she been alone, she would have sat immobile for days, head in hands, and just absorbed the natural tapestry of mille fleur before her.

"Do you really love me?" M'tew asked interrupting her reverie.

Earlier that day, word had gone round the city that a young child had been lost. Within minutes, thousands of the young had gathered in the forum to volunteer to seek for the child. The parents tried vainly to be stoical, yet despite all their outward courage, the inner anxiety was clear for everyone gathered to see, and the collective hearts of the youth of the city went out to the bereft couple.

"Have no fear, we will find him!" was said again and again in hope of offering reassurance to the couple's burdened souls.

The child had wandered off into the plains some hours earlier in chase of a baby fawn. So half of the posse of youth took off in pairs to find the high spots from which they could watch the plains for any movement, whilst the remainder strung out in long lines to tread the undergrowth and explore the gullies, seeking a child perhaps fallen amidst their snares.

M'tew had arrived in the city that morning, stepping off his father's private air transporter to be greeted by an overjoyed Shaa'shesh who had jumped straight into his arms.

"Miss me?" she had asked.

"Not at all" he had teased back at which she had kissed him.

"Miss my kisses then?" she had continued. Coming up for breath, he had wisely nodded. They had then talked briefly about the rest of his family and Shaa'shesh was delighted to hear that his brother had finally found someone to settle down with.

"She is a complete tyrant and scares me witless. Her name is Hela'mesh. Poor Asostos must do everything she asks but as a consequence he has put his partying days behind him and is helping with the estate now. She will be the making of him."

"I am glad. His heart was always in the right place ... and I don't just say that because he fancied me either. He just needed the right motivation to become a good husband and a better man."

"Still insist you chose the right brother?" M'tew asked with a strange gleam in his eyes. For once, Shaa'shesh was serious as she replied solemnly:

"You are the only man I have or will ever love."

But before she could show how much she loved him, they both heard a cry go up for help. A young man rushed into the foyer of the air terminus calling for aid:

"To the forum. There is a child missing. The search will begin soon and all are asked to give, of their charity, their time."

"Where was the child last seen?" Shaa'shesh called out and heard the reply from a distance as the man rushed off to spread his distressing news to those gathering in the other foyers in the terminus:

"On the plains."

Shaa'shesh had not waited for an instant, but rather, grasping M'tew's hand securely, she had dragged him off towards the west gate of the city, and then out onto the Flats. She knew the land well and guided him along hidden paths amidst the rocky outcrops, scrublands and orchards that bordered that sector of the city until they came to the *Hill of Charmant*. Halfway up the hill, she turned sharply to their left towards a solitary mallorn tree and sat down beneath its shade, beckoning for her companion to join her. M'tew turned and gasped: for from her vantage point, they had an uninterrupted view of the entire *Plains of Relish*.

Several hours later, however, and M'tew was very bored. He had hoped for conversation but Shaa'shesh had sat silent, attentive to the constant and compelling call of the natural world before her and vigilant in her quest to find the lost child.

"Do you really love me?" M'tew persisted.

"Why do you ask?"

M'tew paused. He was about to broach a subject that had taxed him ever since the day they had spoken on the *Mount of Eron,* nearly a year earlier. In that year, he had learnt to climb trees for the young disciple; he had also watched from afar as she had grown daily more beautiful and mysterious to him. Time and again, he had wished to be at her side, especially when he had seen her clear distress as she told the story of Za'astra's illness, or had heard how she had nearly drowned in the seas of her childhood. He thought that sometimes he understood her, yet at other times he was totally perplexed at her lack of reason and logic, her laughter in the face of disaster, and her guilt for things that lay outside her control.

Today, she had in all seriousness said that she loved him ... and then ignored him for hours in order to watch the wind gently blow across the chequered fields of blues, greens and gold below. Her love, it seemed to him, was dispassionate and inconsistent.

"You do know that you are spoken of with awe in both the city and the provinces as the most stunningly beautiful woman to ever have graced our planet?"

That got her attention. Shaa'shesh gasped then turned towards him in shock, saying: "You ... you ... you fibber you!"

"I never lie," replied M'tew with dignity. "Nor do I have my head so far up in the clouds that I do not notice how all look at you with love, respect and admiration. For all that is holy, Shaa'shesh, you are very, very beautiful! Did you not know that?"

"No. And I do not believe it. And also I am not sure why you are saying this now?"

"I am telling you this because of something you said to me when we sat looking towards the dolphins playing in the *Bay of Preduinta.* You told me you were too young to decide if we should make love. That it was too early for you to make such a decision. Alas, my love, had I not been so stupefied by your earlier promise of a lifetime of love, I would have told you then how foolish your words were. How can you talk of waiting, of making a decision when you are older? Our planet has only weeks left! There is no getting old for either of us. We have only the here and now."

"Why do you want to make love to me?"

"Are you testing me?" M'tew asked in frustration. Shaa'shesh merely smiled and returned to her contemplation of the plains below.

"Very well. I want to make love with you because you are the most beautiful woman in the world."

"Make love to a picture of me then!" was her stern reply, her eyes remaining steadfast before her. M'tew gulped then persevered:

"I want to make love with you because you are the most intriguing and mysterious person I have ever met."

"If you make love with me then the intrigue and the mystery will be lost," and her eyes remained fixed upon the plains.

"I want to make love with you because I want to hold you in my arms and protect you from all that troubles you."

"I will not be caged," and her eyes still looked ahead unwaveringly.

"I have learnt to climb trees for you!" he said in exasperation.

"You should have learnt to do that many years ago," was her outrageous reply and still her eyes did not turn towards him.

"What is it that I must say?" he finally asked as he conceded defeat.

"You have yet to ask what it is I want?" and M'tew caught the whisper of a wavering wistful smile on her lips as she said this. Suddenly both hope and revelation dawned.

"I want to make love to you because *you* want to make love to me."

"I thought you would never ask," and her eyes turned towards him aflame, leaving him in no doubt that her love for him was far from being dispassionate.

Shaa'shesh reached forward to kiss M'tew then noticed that he was no longer looking into her eyes, but rather had looked away. "Too soon or too passionate!" she thought sadly and for the first time in her life she felt embarrassed. "Have I frightened him off by being too pushy? Does he no longer respect me?"

Nervously, she inspected his face for any sign of rejection and saw a crease of either anger or consternation across his brow. She felt the first pin prick of tears, before M'tew turned her heavy heart inside out and upside down with his next words:

"I think I just saw our lost child!"

"Oh!" Shaa'shesh gasped then started to giggle as she realised what a fool she had been. "This love thing is way too complicated for me," she thought to herself then turned to see what had attracted her lover's attention. Next she laughed out loud:

"That is not a child! That is Mr Stoat returning to his family with their supper."

"How on earth can you see a stoat from this distance? I can barely make out the movement of the bushes."

"There is so much I must teach you, my love," and Shaa'shesh smiled then took his hand in her own and held it to her cheek as she continued: "and so little time to tell you it all. I saw the stoat's footprints on our path as we came here and also noticed a bird nesting nearby. The marks told me there was a family of stoats, including young pups. Whilst if you listen carefully you will hear that the birds are singing contentedly and not raising an alarm. Therefore, the birds have sensed a familiar presence and not that of a stranger. It is Mr Stoat as I have said. Anyone else and the birds would have given them away."

But Shaa'sehsh had seen something else and now it was her turn to stiffen and look attentively into the distance. Far across the valley was a herd of wild horses, but it was not this that had drawn her attention, rather their companion.

For standing in the middle of the herd and looking directly towards her was a magnificent stag.

"Come on! It is time for you to meet an old friend of mine. It seems he has something to tell me," and she strode off down into the valley with a bemused M'tew in tow.

As they walked the hidden paths of the valley below, the sun dipped its head and, in departing grace, turned the valley briefly into crimson flame, before the bright silver of the crescent Pallas and the approaching asteroid, their twin moons mirrored in the glazed golden and coruscating copper surface of Mnesis' many rings, ablaze in the silent silken sky overhead, provided the guiding light for Shaa'shesh and her faithful companion.

M'tew was constantly amazed at Shaa'shesh's knowledge of the Flats, as she unerringly guided him through scrubland and forest, across hidden fords and via ancient paths into the depths of the *Plains of Relish*.

They passed through waterfalls that had turned to ice, to provide a ghost-like reflection of the two questers, causing M'tew to shiver with temporary fright at the silvery spectres they had become, whilst Shaa'shesh just laughed.

Wading through the warm verdant waters of the *River Fleurin,* the couple stood atop the stone carrack at the centre of the white-sanded deserted valley of *Vespas* to watch the absorption of the night-time rain, and the explosion of multi-coloured plant life, that was this valley's delighted response to the daily gift of moisture.

Traversing the terrifying *Chasm of Perdition*, once the causeway for a mighty river that had since sunk beneath the permeable rock many hundreds of feet below them, they used the inter-twined fronds of the ancient Redhorn trees to swing precariously from one tall bank to the other.

Throughout the journey, Shaa'shesh would point out new stars and constellations to her souls-mate, each described by her through their unique story and as a living entity. In the brief moments when the clouds covered the bejewelled tapestry of the cosmos, she would turn their attention to the scurrying and scavenging wildlife, showing M'tew the sets of badgers and foxes, the watery holes of rats, voles and moles, the trail of toads, the burrows of rabbits, the marches of hares, and the mesne of deer. The birds were silent, save for the occasional questioning hoot of an owl, but soon M'tew began to understand the whispered language of this night-time land: muted and yet distinct, he realised that even as the people of Mnesis slept, their world was still alive to the beauty but also the insistent and constant task of being natural.

Finally, M'tew asked Shaa'shesh the question that had been burning within him since the day they had re-met at his father's mansion:

"Tell me about the Creator. You talk of him or her as someone real, someone with whom you converse. Yet, to me, this is madness or derangement. The world we see is the result of the laws of physics, of DNA and RNA created out of some cosmic explosion many eons ago. I know you understand this and yet you also follow the promptings of something else? I would understand you better, my love, so tell me how you converse with your Creator."

Shaa'shesh looked into M'tew's eyes and saw the seriousness of the question writ large within them. She did not hesitate, but beckoned for him to sit by her side and then holding one of his hands gently for reassurance, looked up into the sky and spoke from her heart and her soul:

"I believe in the Creator because I see too much of beauty and order around me to believe this is *randomly* created. I also believe that the first origins of our universe were designed. I have yet to find the evidence in my studies of the universe of anything that sits outside the rules that govern us, such as gravity, to suggest anything other than we live in a set of worlds that have been ordained by rules. I believe in a rule setter, therefore. A being of such power and authority that he or she was able to bind the cosmos to a composition, a concerto that has stood the test of time and that still governs the dance and the story that is the stars.

"I also believe that my beliefs will not convince anyone. That conversion is something left to the special relationship that the Creator seeks with every one of us. There is no single path to that relationship - we cannot confine or cage the Creator in that way. Rather *the Path* is individually designed to reflect the unique choices we all make in life. I believe therefore that the Creator will discover us *all* one day, whatever path we choose, and that the Creator can also make the path we have chosen *become* the right path.

"My conversations with the Creator are the hardest to describe. On almost all occasions, it is like a whisper at the end of a corridor, and as you head towards the words their sound grows further away, the words remain at the edge of perception, you cannot be certain of what you have heard, as he or she who spoke the words has turned the next corner, and thus you follow again and again but never quite touch or see the speaker. It is like the most distant of echoes in the mountains, a muffled sound that can be distorted, their direction hidden, yet the sound can also be distinct, almost imperative in its ferocity one moment, and then fade to obscurity the next. I can never be certain that I have understood the words correctly; so must also follow my heart as well as my head ... which is just as well as my head has this habit of sending me into the most terrible scrapes.

"On three occasions, however, I have felt the presence of the Creator. On each, it is my belief, the Creator wished to be present to reinforce the import of what I was being asked to do or being told. Thus, I heard with compelling clarity of *my mission*, *my innocence* of my father's death, and *my need* to serve the Master. My purpose was strengthened on those occasions by both the physical presence of a messenger sent by the Creator and by the reinforcement of the Creator's will within my heart, mind and soul."

"You have endured much. Seen and lived through great sadness and much stress. Can you not be certain that your visions or sense of the presence of the Creator are not the delusions of a tired and over-wrought mind?" M'tew asked tentatively, aware he risked their recent declarations of love but wanting to ensure their relationship was founded on the bedrock of truth.

Shaa'shesh surprised him once more by having one of her fits of the giggles. Curling into a ball, she just rolled around on the ground in hoots of laughter before eventually getting her breath back enough to say simply:

"I don't think with my head. I think with my heart. Of course I may have delusions. I am probably quite mad. But that is all up in my head somewhere and I have never taken any notice of all that nonsense. No. I am pure passion and senses and not a lot else. If I ever stopped to think, well heaven help us all, is all I can say!"

The curtain of the trees parted, and the couple stood beneath a clouded black sky atop a solitary grassy knoll to look down upon a strand of total stillness and darkness.

"Where are we?" M'tew asked with a shiver at the emptiness of this place, in stark contrast to all he had seen in the preceding hours.

"A very special place. Close your eyes to take in the scent of this place and all will become clear."

M'tew did as directed. What greeted him was the sharp, almost citrus, tang that comes when in the presence of pure, ice cold, crystal clear water. All his fears disappeared as he realised the dark strand before him was a lake, and from its distinctive bouquet, one of such purity of composition that he was wary to approach it for risk of polluting it. He opened his eyes, just as the clouds parted above his head, and his revelation was answered as the lake before him lit up with the perfect reflection of the panoply of the moon, advancing asteroid and the stars: black waters forming the background to an intricate necklace of gleaming diamonds that floated ethereally on its still surface.

"Watch!" Shaa'shesh whispered reverently.

As they did so, a ring of new stars appeared as if by magic at the water's edge. M'tew was astounded; scarce able to understand how such stars could come into being in this way at the command of his companion.

All his knowledge of science and nature was briefly overcome and over-whelmed. He looked up into the skies, yet could not see the mirror image of these new stars in the heavens above him, and so remained confused, afraid even, at this insight that the laws of physics were not the sole ordinance of the cosmos!

Shaa'shesh looked at him lovingly, read the bemusement in his eyes, saw the direction of his confused glance, and broke the solemnity of their silence with her gay laugh:

"They are the reflection of eyes, silly, not stars. This is whom we have come to meet."

The conflagration of a new dawn greeted them, its crimson tendrils, as dragon's fire, curling, twisting and engulfing the stars, the fading twin moons receding before the coruscation of its flame, as dark sapphire-blue night-time turned to blazing white and then the gentle cyan of cloudless sky. Fiery red burned briefly across the mirror of the lake, cleansing its obsidian of all reflection, to reveal waters so clean that the creams and gold of the stones on its bed were clearly visible to the two watchers.

In the very centre of the lake was an island, with a solitary tree, attached to the lakeside by the narrowest of causeways. M'tew's eyes were drawn inexorably towards the island. Not because of its beauty, nor its sense of mysterious isolation, but rather because standing at its very edge was the most powerful and magnificent animal, he had ever seen. Around the lake's banks were arrayed herd upon herd of deer: bucks and does gathered in homage to honour he whom stood in commanding pride on the island.

Shaa'shesh bowed then smiled as she called across the waters:

"Hello, LeCerf. I need your help."

The mightiest of stags bowed its noble head briefly to acknowledge the girl's request, its antlers of many seasons adorned with four tiers of sharpened horn, each showing the remnants of bloody battles to demonstrate its mastery over the herds of deer that followed him.

Then, he added to M'tew's amazement at the new discoveries of nature he had already made that day by replying to the girl's simple request:

"Is this the buck you have chosen? Shall I test him with my horns? You choose *this* weakling over me?"

"Hush, my dear friend. Yes, I have chosen him. Already he has made me very happy to be in his company. But there is no need of jealousy here. He offers no threat."

LeCerf tossed his great head briefly as if imagining M'tew at the mercy of his antlers but then reared back and laughed:

"That you are happy makes me so, also. And I can see he poses no threat!" at which they both looked towards M'tew who was trying desperately to hide behind a tree at this point, "But I shall still hope for the day when you will join the sanctity and protection of my herd."

"I think you and I know that the day approaches soon when we shall *all* be gathered to our Father's Place, to become one in his presence, to be part of the same herd, to see nature and humanity as one," the girl replied philosophically, curtseying to LeCerf as she did so. At which the stag placed his left foreleg forward and returned her bow in honour at her wise words.

"Ask for my aid, pure-hearted one. It shall be granted."

"We seek a child who is lost by name of Perditus."

"The child is **not** lost," the stag replied. "Rather, he has seen a thing that this world had missed and through the goodness of his heart he has sought to put right by himself. Though small, though young, he is a sensitive child and he understands the meaning of the phrase:' he who sees a problem is often in the right place to resolve it.'

Ensure he is not chastised for his absence, for his actions serve us all well and are to be commended."

"What is it he has achieved?" Shaa'shesh asked in both astonishment but also relief at the news that the child was safe.

"I shall show you. To see shall be simpler and offer more explanation than to tell. Will you ride on my back as you did as a small child?"

"Gladly," and the girl smiled at the childhood memories of such rides, then suddenly she recalled the presence of M'tew: "I am not so certain M'tew will enjoy the experience though?"

"He must stay here. My herds will guard him, but he is not ready yet for the honour of being carried by any of us. One day, perhaps, he shall prove his love for nature and creation is greater than his love for science. Until that day, he is tolerated by us but not as yet loved."

So, Shaa'shesh mounted the strong shoulders of LeCerf to be carried on the safety of his back, as her lover waited nervously by the side of the *Lake Blackwater.* The stag flew at great speed, in chase of the wind it seemed, and the land beneath his hooves flew by, league upon league. The girl did not question her mount or seek any answer to where they were heading, trusting implicitly that her antlered companion would deliver her to the lost child.

Instead, they spoke of times distant and to come, of fears and hopes, of nature's ability to create and destroy.

"Is our world's end certain?" asked the stag and Shaa'shesh sighed deeply, before replying:

"It is the question we have asked the Master to resolve and he has told us that the physical end of our world is indeed certain. Yet he speaks of hope."

"What hope can there be for a world that shall end?"

"We can be remembered ... with love. We can serve a more noble purpose: to have saved a new world. We can set that world an example: of tolerance and respect; of peace and harmony with nature; the union of science and the divine. This is my hope."

LeCerf turned his head towards her at this, in awe at her vision but also for the first time understanding the incredible scope of the mission that she had set herself. Then with the shadow of emotion in the gruffness of his voice, he bellowed:

"You shall never be forgotten, my dear! Now prepare for the ride of your life, for the child is not far."

She did not have long to wait, for within the hour they came to a secreted grove, on the banks of a shimmering stream, beneath the canopy of bending birches and proud prunus, in the shadow of gently sloping chalk hills. Amidst the trees was a place of calm, where the bounteous beauty of spring flowers had burst forth in clusters of yellow and white narcissi, the blues and reds of tulips, and the soft carpet of pink blossom, fallen from two mated plum trees, displaying their love with the gift of their rose-coloured bloom.

Seated in the centre of the grove was a young child surrounded by birds and small mammals of every type and species, each one seeking comfort from the gentle stirring and caress of his small hands.

LeCerf bowed forward on his forelegs to allow Shaa'shesh to dismount and then watched her approach the young boy carefully, for she did not wish to disturb the peaceful idyll she saw. The child was not to be distracted and his companions continued to muster to his careful attentions. None noticed her quiet approach. In the end, she turned towards the stag, questioningly, to whisper:

"Is it a spell?"

"No, my dear delight. It is a blessing. The child has appreciated what your whole world has not yet seen: that we, the animals of this world, are **frightened**. The wondrous changes you see in the seasons and the weather across this world, caused by the approaching doom of the asteroid, have become something terrifyingly strange to those brought up to rely on the constancy of the seasons. The child has realised that we, the birds of the air, the fishes of the sea, the animals of the land, need something ... we need your comfort."

Shaa'shesh gasped. How stupid she had been not to see this for herself, how selfish! She turned towards LeCerf and laughing, made the stag a promise:

"I shall tell my people. All shall know we must do as Perditus. He has shown us through his simple love and generosity of heart an example that every young person shall respect, honour and seek to follow. Better we live these last days comforting those who are afraid, than we sit back as the spectators of the demise of our world. But tell me, my friend, will Perditus come home with me?"

"Ask him."

Shaa'shesh stepped forward gingerly and sat beside the child. First, she offered her hands to the young animals that surrounded him and they, recognising her inherent gentleness and compassion, nuzzled her fingers and then sat on her lap. Perditus paused in his own careful comforting of his companions to turn and smile his gratitude for her aid in his self-commissioned task. Now having the child's attention, Shaa'shesh returned his smile reassuringly then asked:

"If you will come with me, I think I can find many friends who will help you comfort the animals. Not just in this place, but in every place where they seek out our comfort."

The child paused in thought and then nodded.

Thus it was that the ninth story to be included on the disc that would one day be sent to the safety of the planetoid Pallas, as a testimony to the people of Mnesis, **was the story of a young child who understood that the animals of his world needed comfort in the face of the terrors of a dying planet.**

M'tew took Shaa'shesh back to the *Hills of Charmant* and made gentle love with her as she had always wished. In their joy and passion in each other, the doom of any number of approaching asteroids might just as well have been at the furthest ends of the universe for all that they cared.

Chapter Eleven: Nar'csa

Ptere'an was pacing up and down on the glass balcony of his apartment overlooking the amphitheatre in the *Bibliotechnaoi*. He was close to being overwhelmed with a mixture of new emotions: frustration (almost desperation) that with three weeks to go, he was still three stories short of the Master's target, mingled with ongoing concern over his daughter's deteriorating health.

Somehow Za'astra hung on to life, yet the medical attendants were unable to offer any long term hopeful prognosis.

Shaa'shesh watched the spectacle of Ptere'an's pacing from her perch on the chrome rail that ran from one end of the balcony to the other, her feet swinging precariously some 100 metres from the ground beneath, adding fear for her safety, had she but known it, to the melange of feelings competing within Ptere'an's beleaguered mind. In the end, he could not bear it anymore and exclaimed:

"Shaa'shesh, please be careful, you might fall!"

"I might fly too," she laughed. "And you might solve our world's problems by marching up and down like an automaton! You might even wear a hole in the balcony floor and fall through. But instead, I suggest a hug and then you can tell me what is worrying you. Listening to you is much more fun than watching you torture yourself for no reason, my friend."

At which, she stood up and tiptoed along the rail, causing Ptere'an to start forward in horror, until he realised she was teasing him.

Only when he was seated sedately in his great leather chair before his carved oak desk, did the girl jump off the rail and come over to give him the promised hug:

"Much better," she smiled. "Now talk and I will listen ... and behave myself too."

"Where am I to find the last stories for the Master?" Ptere'an began, placing his worries over the task he had been given before his own personal fears, but Shaa'shesh knew her friend better than this and placing a finger on his lips, silenced him briefly before saying:

"Tell me about Za'astra."

At last the tears came. Shaa'shesh held Ptere'an tight in her arms as he unburdened all the fears and concerns of a loving father with no-one else to talk to:

"I cannot tell my wife any of this as she is being so brave herself, yet we both see the possibility of future loss in each other's eyes and have no way to communicate this to each other. We are afraid that we shall each take away the other's strength. But I have so wanted to talk about Za'astra to someone. The physicians just want to talk about her health; I want to talk about her life and her hopes ... and my hopes for her."

Shaa'shesh nodded in encouragement for Ptere'an to continue but she remained silent, knowing this time he needed her company and not her words.

"To be fair, since you have been coming to see her, her health is stable. She does not recover, but she is no longer growing weak. I am so grateful for this, and should have told you before, that your presence in our house is a blessing."

Shaa'shesh was having none of this, however, and pinched him playfully, forcing Ptere'an to grin in response, before he carried on unburdening himself:

"No-one knows yet, however, what ails her. It is some new disease. So she sits and watches nature unfold through her bedroom window, without hope of recovery. It comes near to breaking my heart for I would have her well and playing in the gardens she watches so avidly."

"Can she not sit in the gardens?" Shaa'shesh asked meditatively.

Ptere'an paused then began to nod with growing intensity. Indeed, as Shaa'shesh watched him carefully from beneath half-closed eye lids, a gleam of appreciation in her eyes, she saw the stone that was in his character return to give him strength and purpose:

"You have a day bed. Can I borrow it? I am certain if I ask my neighbours, they will agree to my setting it up in their gardens."

"I suspect they have been waiting daily for you to ask!" and Shaa'shesh laughed. "The bed is yours. I have never slept in it after all. Set it up in a different garden each day. And play with Za'astra. It is her father she wants more than the gardens. She watches those gardens as she imagines herself playing **with you** in them. Give your daughter her hopes and her dreams and you will fulfil your own also."

"But my work?" exclaimed Ptere'an, torn momentarily between the wonderful prospect of time with his daughter and the commitment he had made to the Master.

"Blah! I will find you a story. Now take the rest of the week off and do something useful for a change."

Nar'csa had the rarest of colourings for her people and as a consequence was held in high regard ... and yet she also stood apart. Red or purple hair, green eyes and grey-blue skin were common-place amongst her peers - her own family were no different in this regard. Yet, somehow her normal parents had given birth to a daughter with fair creamy skin, blue eyes and blonde hair.

Nar'csa had been accepted with love by a people whose culture and values revolved around tolerance and respect for each other's differences. She was offered admiration for her distinctive looks, deemed wondrously beautiful by those who met her, but in her own mind she was inferior; her poor opinion of herself kept her distant from her family and those with whom she studied as a child. She grew up silent and reflective, yet always helpful to those she saw in need.

One week before Ptere'an decided to take time off to be with his daughter, and Shaa'shesh had made her rash promise to find a story for him, Nar'csa had stood on a rock at the edge of the great lake *Ch'rion* to look into its crystal clear, mirror-like waters at the reflection she saw before her ... and from that moment onwards had remained transfixed.

At first, her parents had been heartened that their daughter had finally seen the beauty in her looks that they had always appreciated, but as the hours of her fascination had turned into days and then into a week without movement from her spot by the lakeside, they (and the others who lived in their humble village by the lake) began to see her inaction as unnatural.

Self-love was healthy, but to devote so much time unproductively in the contemplation of one's own fair looks was unheard of. They feared for Nar'csa's mental health, yet none dared try and move her, as it was contrary to their ethos to impose their will on another in this way. Instead, a crowd gathered each day in fascination to watch the young girl, to pity her, to keep her company, but also to wish she would somehow break the spell that her own reflection had cast upon her.

M'tew was watching Shaa'shesh doing a handstand on Ptere'an's desk. Smiling, he could not help asking:

"And how precisely is doing that going to help you find the next story? More importantly, what came over you to make such a rash and idiotic promise to Ptere'an?"

"Ptere'an looks for too much depth and sophistication in the stories he would collect. He sets the bar too high in my view. For every story we have finally selected so far has been simple – *yet come from an unexpected direction*. Standing on my head, I am much more likely to see the important things for our planet and our people *from a fresh perspective*."

"Seen anything yet worth telling me about?"

At which Shaa'shesh blushed then laughed, before admitting grudgingly:

"You look just as gorgeous upside down! And as soon as that thought came into my head that is all I have been able to think about for the last few minutes. Now can you help me down as I am feeling rather giddy?"

M'tew caught her in his strong arms as she tumbled off the desk, snatched a quick kiss whilst she was still disorientated, then plonked her down in Ptere'an's burgundy leather revolving admiral's chair. She took a few moments to get her breath back, then started to spin the chair round clockwise then anticlockwise, her legs out straight before her.

M'tew looked up at the ceiling in exasperation at her inability to sit still for the briefest of moments and Shaa'shesh, catching him in the act, stuck her tongue out at him, or at least tried too but was already quite boss-eyed, then laughed once more, somewhat ruefully this time:

“I know what you are thinking. I should be reflecting on the task that I have been given. Yet all I can do is dance, sing, jump, run, do handstands, spin round or do anything but be still. But it is my belief, my dearest delight, that the next story will come here and find me and not the other way around.”

M’tew just shook his head in despair at the madcap disciple who had given herself so passionately to him only days earlier and with whom he intended to be paired formally before the finality of Mnesis’ destruction. Moments later, his jaw came close to dropping to the floor in astonishment when there was a knock on the door and one of Ptere’an’s staff popped her head in to announce:

“Kr’sten and Pers’eplis have come from the village of *Grav’ston* by the lake *Ch’rion* to seek Shaa’shesh’s advice. They are concerned about their daughter Nar’csa and wondered if the Master’s favourite disciple would be able to offer some insight or revelation into the affliction that besets their much-loved child.”

“Show them in, I was just telling M’tew that I was expecting them,” Shaa’shesh replied, desperately avoiding any eye contact with M’tew for fear it would set her off giggling at his utter amazement and confusion.

“Either you already knew these people were coming or you are incredibly lucky!” M’tew muttered whilst they waited for Nar’csa’s parents to be shown in.

“Neither! One day I must teach you about *faith*. This interview may mean nothing, but my heart tells me this is our next story. Even if it is not, I would still wish to offer my aid to these people for they have come to ask for my help and how can I refuse?”

Kr’sten and Pers’eplis were humble net makers, from a small village half a continent away from the capital of *Persepolis.* Pers’eplis’ name told Shaa’shesh that the lady was an orphan, named after the capital where she would have been taken in as a child, as was the custom amongst those unfortunate enough to have lost their birthparents and not to be adopted. Kr’sten was a strong and handsome man, whose family had never left his village, or the trade that he now continued with the willing aid of his wife.

The couple had met by fate or accident twenty years earlier when Pers’eplis, a sixteen year old orphan on her first field trip beyond the boundaries of the capital that had been her constant home until that point, had stood and looked at the ice tipped, obsidian mountains of *Ty'roc*, standing majestically over the forests of *Cali'phur* and mirrored in perfect symmetrical reflection within the still waters of the *Ch'rion.*

The view had mesmerised her ... its contemplation had also meant that she had missed her rendezvous with the rest of those on the outing and been stranded by the black and silver waters of the lake.

Kr'sten had spent a long day repairing nets. He was in his twenties yet worked alone as the solitary remaining member of a declining business, struggling as the fishing trade had collapsed, but that had continued uninterrupted in the village of *Grav'ston* for over four hundred years. Eleven years ago, the fishing trade may have imploded but even today there was still a market for nets as decorative items and as safety nets on the ships that braved the tempests of the seas.

Many years ago, he had lost both of his parents and his only brother in a storm upon the lake as they had gone out to fish, returning with laiden nets into the head of a freak tempest, rushing furiously straight from the terrors of *Ty'roc*.

The weight of the nets had dragged their small trawler to the bed of the lake in less than a minute, before they had been able to cut the nets from their moorings.

On the day, Kr'sten met Pers'eplis, he had already got behind with many orders for new nets and for repairs of existing nets. He knew his trade was important to the rest of the village, yet the work involved was unexciting compared with the opportunity to take the many tourists by boat onto the lake itself. He had no volunteers to aid him and found himself working longer and longer hours yet slipping further and further behind with his order book. Bereft of the aid of a family, he feared his vulnerable business would soon flounder.

Taking a walk along the lakeside, in order to free up the cramps in his thighs and arms from a long day's labour before retiring to his lonely cabin, he had heard Pers'eplis' tears of fear as the young girl contemplated sleeping in a dark and strange place, many leagues from the orphanage that had been her home, and without hope of shelter.

At first sight, the girl had fallen heart and soul for the dark handsome and strong man, her saviour and shining gallant knight. Just as importantly, he represented her way out of the orphanage that was her current abode and her chance to set up her nest by the *Ch'rion* with the sight of which she had also fallen in love.

Kr'sten in turn was smitten by her beauty and vulnerability ... only later would he discover her strength of purpose and willingness and aptitude for new skills that would rescue his business, as he had rescued her that first night they had met.

Within a few days of their meeting, Pers'eplis had taken charge of the order book, doing what Kr'sten had been too busy to do himself and ensuring that each task was done in the order it needed to be undertaken to ensure that as many nets as possible would be completed on time. For orders she knew they could not complete to time, she met with those customers in person and agreed a revised date. Most stood by their local net-maker, accepting the delay in the return of their damaged nets, and only a few transferred their business to the competition in the next village.

After four weeks she had learnt enough from observing Kr'sten to help make new nets – repairs were far more complex so were left to Kr'sten. But having a second pair of hands for new orders meant that they were able to catch up with the waiting list that had developed, go back to some of their long-standing clients and bring the delivery date for their nets forward, guaranteeing future business from them.

For Kr'sten, finding Pers'eplis had become the miracle that had saved his family business and he took the opportunity to pair with her, discovering to his amazement a willing partner, who was head over heels in love with him and the spectacular view from his cabin, set on the banks of her beloved *Ch'rion*.

Soon, they were gifted with three sons and four daughters, all of whom helped with the net-making and the business had grown to take on that of four neighbouring villages.

Nar'csa was their youngest daughter, being just fifteen when she stood on the lonely rock by the banks of the *Ch'rion* and fell into her trance. She was very much their favourite, despite or because of her strange looks. Nar'csa's lack of self-esteem had concerned her parents deeply but led them to offer her more love and to spend more time with her.

As the couple had contemplated the beauty of their surroundings, she would be their constant companion when they took their night-time stroll along the banks of the lake.

Nar'csa had always been the first to volunteer to do any long shift on the nets and equally would go to the aid of anyone struck ill or needing help, sleeping over with many of the elderly in the village to offer them the security of her quiet company and assist them in the early hours of the morning. Yet she communicated little except to smile sadly as she got on with her work or lent her gentle strength to an unsteady neighbour.

The couple were aware from their other daughters that there was stage as they grew up when they could become overly conscious of their own looks. It was usually a passing phase and had seen their other girls spend a few hours each day in front of the mirror thinking about how to enhance their looks with make-up, a new hair style, jewellery or clothing.

But they had never encountered anyone who would just stand and look at their reflection for days on end without food or drink in such silent awe. This had to be unnatural! It was also all the more surprising given Nar'csa's own previously disparaging view of her appearance.

Nar'csa's parents had concluded that either their daughter was unwell, deranged even, or a spell had been cast over her, and thus they had come to the capital to seek help. Unsure to whom to turn to for assistance, they had gone to the *Bibliotechnaoi*, the place of all knowledge. There, they had learnt of the name and reputation of Shaa'shesh from those who were in study or participating in the *story feste*.

Kr'sten had told their story briefly, in simple words, Pers'eplis nodding occasionally or adding a thoughtful additional detail, but clearly the couple were in awe of their surroundings, and in particular the stunning view of the capital which was the backdrop to their interview.

Shaa'shesh had asked only one question "Tell me how you met and why you have come?" and then sat in silence, for once not moving an inch to avoid disturbing the account that they gave. At the end of their story, she sighed, before saying to them both reassuringly and with her gentle compassionate smile:

"I can help. Have no fear for your daughter. You must take me to her."

Ptere'an's secretariat organised for the necessary air transporter to take Shaa'shesh, M'tew (who insisted on coming), Kr'sten and Pers'eplis to Lake *Ch'rion*. They used Ptere'an's name, his important office and standing, to book a time slot in the busy schedule at the space port that would see the Master's private air transporter take off in less than an hour from the end of the interview and arrive at *Ch'rion* a mere 35 minutes later (a journey that had taken Nar'csa's parents over three days coming by public air transport).

The nearest clearing to where Nar'csa kept her constant vigil to the reflection of her own looks was just over two miles away from the lake and the terrain between was both dense forest and full of rocky gullies and rills. Even with the expert help, guidance and local knowledge of Nar'csa's parents, the group would take over seven hours to traverse those two miles. It would be dark when they arrived.

"Good! I am relieved" laughed Shaa'shesh. "There will still be the light of our moon and more importantly there will be no crowd of spectators, the sight of which might embarrass Nar'csa when she comes out of her 'enchantment'."

It was the early hours of the morning when the four had finally arrived at the banks of the *Ch'rion*, the solitary rock by the shore line that was Nar'csa's viewing point clearly visible in the bright moon light. The lake reflected its surroundings in silver and deep blue, the sight of which took Shaa'shesh's breath away. Nar'csa stood motionless on the edge of the rock, her head looking downwards toward her reflection in the water.

"Has anyone approached her or tried to move her?"

"No" replied Kr'sten sternly. "To move her against her will would be undignified and disrespectful. If this is the help you offer then we must ask you to leave."

Shaa'shesh laughed at this and then replied: "Trust me! I have more respect for your daughter than even you," then before Kr'sten could stop her, she ran towards the rock.

She had the element of surprise and she was also very light and fleet of foot, so reached the rock before Kr'sten could catch her up. But she did not touch Nar'csa. Rather she stood next to her and carefully looked into the girl's eyes to see where Nar'csa was looking.

Then placing herself alongside the girl, she looked out into the lake to the same spot and saw ...

... not her own reflection, nor that of Nar'csa, but the reflection of the stars and the moon, the mountains, the forests and the surrounding countryside.

She turned to the panting Kr'sten at the foot of the rock and said:

"You are not the first nor will you be the last to accuse someone of self contemplation, self-admiration, of narcissism, because they are silent and reflective. It is too easy for those of us who lack imagination or who are active in our own lives to consider those who spend time in reflection or contemplation as being self-absorbed.

"When we make such accusations, however, we are assuming that what they reflect on is themselves through an excess of self-love. Yet how can we be certain of this unless we stand where they stand and look where they look?

"Your daughter is not mesmerised by her own reflection. She is in mourning and saying goodbye to the beauty of her surroundings. A love for which she has learnt from you, her parents, and rightly so. Her love for what she sees should be praised not pitied. Many of her age have sought money, the good life, to enjoy the last days of our planet in an orgy of materialism. Your daughter has chosen the better path: to say farewell in silent awe at the majesty of our Creator's design.

"Continue to be proud of her, for she loves what matters. Her love for you both will bring her back to you."

"What should I do?" Kr'sten asked in chagrin, remorse and self-doubt.

"Stand beside her and tell her you love her. She will remember then that there are things of beauty to be cherished that are more than a beautiful reflection in a moon-lit lake."

Kr'sten clambered up the rock and stood carefully to the left of his daughter, with Shaa'shesh to her right, ready to catch Nar'csa should she fall forward as the spell of the reflection on the lake wore off.

"Nar'csa," said the contrite man "I love you and find you more beautiful even than the wonderful reflection you see before you. You were made by the Creator, as were the mountains before you, but for me you are the greater of his works. I ask in these last days of our world that we spend as much time together as we can. I ask you come back to me."

"I can see your reflection father and it gives me great joy," was his daughter's whispered response, speaking for the first time in nearly ten days.

"Would you let *the real* me hold you in my arms rather than just my reflection?"

The girl nodded and with tears in her eyes turned and allowed him to hold her. Gradually she relaxed as she was comforted by the strength in his arms, then looked up with sparkling eyes and smiled:

"I love you more than anything I have seen in this world father, real or reflection. But I had to say goodbye to the land that brought you and my mother together. Forgive me my time of contemplation, but also be happy that I am returned now and with the benefit of the revelation that the last ten days have given me. For it is my belief that a reflection of our world of Mnesis will survive the apocalypse we all face."

Thus it was that the tenth story to be recorded on the disc and placed in the casket destined to be set in safety upon the orbiting Pallas was of **a girl who was mistakenly thought to be narcissistic but who was actually privately mourning the passing of her beautiful world**

As Nar'csa told her people about her dream of a world like Mnesis, but that would live beyond the destruction of their home, the approaching asteroid above their heads seemed to grow ever more distant.

Chapter Twelve: Shaa'shesh

Shaa'shesh shook with the first heat of the fever that had swept through the gathered crowds in *Paraclemos*, decimating her gentle and vulnerable people, only weeks before their world was due to come to an abrupt end in collision with the asteroid that now hung as a great golden globe in the daytime sky for all to see.

It was a cruel irony that her world should be struck down by plague, and thus be unable to meet the doom of their planet with the courage and dignity that had been their original plan.

Hundreds were already dead, including all of her friends that she had gathered during her days of homelessness when as a teenager she had wandered the streets of *Paraclemos*, a few pennies to her name earned from her dancing and singing performances in the street theatre of the citadel, but attracting many companions through her bright vision of hope for a future for her people.

Those who followed her had become the Master's first disciples, her gift to Sala'am when Shaa'shesh and he had met: a promise of light in his darkest moment when he had begun to despair of ever finding an answer to the doom of his race.

Without argument or hesitation, the disciples had fed the crowds that had flocked to the *Bibliotechnaoi*, spreading the word of the Master's vision, and making the vain attempt to heal those who fell foul of the disease tearing through the people of Mnesis. Thus, they had also caught the plague, as Shaa'shesh had, through contact with those who initially succumbed, and her closest friends had become amongst the first to perish.

Shaa'shesh was the last of the Master's disciples still alive.

With the death of her friends and companions, there were only a few carers left to help the growing ranks of the unwell, whilst the scientists of Mnesis predicted that the virus would slay every living person on the planet within a fortnight, and without hope of any cure. The majority of the population of Mnesis had taken to their homes, hiding away, awaiting death in fearful solitude. The streets were now quiet and deserted, whilst the Master's *story feste* had been rapidly abandoned for the risk it presented through personal contact.

Shaa'shesh refused to die in her bed, however unwell she might feel. Nothing would stop her spending her last moments in the company and serenity of the trees that had been her greatest love and provided her with a place of solace from the impending tragedy of her planet's end. Ignoring the protests from her masked carer, she flung back the sheets then took a few staggering steps to the window to look out on the forested hills to the north of the city. She sighed.

Ptere'an knocked tentatively. Shaa'shesh was already beyond the early stages of the plague, when it was at is most virulent and contagious; and it was still too early in its progress for the respiratory and cardiac failure that marked the final stages of the disease. The girl could therefore receive visitors without risk of the contagion spreading ... but Ptere'an was not sure if she would wish any company to see her looking so frail. More than that, he felt an overwhelming sense of guilt that his friend should have contracted the plague from contact with his own daughter, Za'astra. His daughter, miraculously, still lived, but at what cost he pondered as he looked across at his fragile friend?

Shaa'shesh's smile of relief at sight of him was all the reassurance he needed to step quietly into the room, and sit by her vacated bed, as she clung to the glass, her nose pressed against the window, wishing herself elsewhere.

"They will not let me go and climb a tree," whispered the girl, sadly, then remembering her manners turned and grinned at Ptere'an, before continuing: "which is why you are going to find a way to smuggle me out of here!"

Ptere'an blinked and then listened as she chattered on gaily, reminiscing:

"Did I ever tell you that I was climbing up a tree when I first met the Master? He seemed so alone, lost even. I considered telling him to join me, as I have found that climbing a tree can solve many problems and remove all my concerns. But instead we spoke and from my words he seemed to gain confidence. He has sought me out for advice or comfort ever since, that is until these last few months when he has been shut away in our Space Port at *Melchor*. I have been so lonely Ptere'an ... and that is why I need the company of my trees."

"If you think that I am going to smuggle you out of this Medical Centre, then you are sadly delusional! And none of your usual blackmail is going to convince me otherwise, my girl. I am far too used to your tricks by now for any of them to work on me."

Shaa'shesh giggled and then stuck her tongue out at him, a tongue aflame with purple and green spots. But for a moment she did not care, whilst Ptere'an had seen the same signs of the plague in his daughter. Knowing that the disciple had caught the disease from the single kiss of reassurance she had given Za'astra a few weeks earlier, he masked the guilt of that memory, by seeking a way to distract them both and thus found himself asking:

"You have never told your life story. Indeed, you are probably the only person I know save the Master yet to do so. It would honour me greatly to hear it. And not just me, I think, but our whole world has waited to hear of your origins, your past, your present and your hopes for the future. You are much loved and also much in people's hearts at the moment."

The girl smiled wistfully but she could refuse her friend nothing. He was so much a part of her life now that his every request was an imperative. She had her own priorities, however, and so her initial response was a question of her own:

"How is M'tew?"

"Miraculously, he has not contracted the disease despite his constant contact with those who have. He spends every waking moment seeking remedy amongst those who are dying of the plague. He quests for a cure … he seeks to save *you* and despairs that he lives in health whilst you do not."

"You are well also? Za'astra still lives?"

"Yes to both. My daughter's survival remains a constant benison of hope for us all. If anything she is gaining in health, because of or despite the care she receives. But she misses you greatly; her tears for you break my heart."

Shaa'shesh's eyes shone brightly at the news of Za'astra's and M'tew's good health. She took a deep breath in preparation to tell her life story, coughed, rasping as she remembered how stupid that was for her to do in her condition, began to chuckle, lost her balance, keeled over, her remaining breath departing, gasped, laughed, collapsed, and fell out of bed. Alarms went off on several monitors and two care attendants rushed in to see what had happened.

"Sorry" the poor girl whispered as they shook their heads at her, reset the monitors, glared at Ptere'an, and admonished them both to behave:

"This girl is *ill* so take care of her as she has no idea how to look after herself!" was their parting shot at Ptere'an as they left Shaa'shesh's room again.

"Well, where to begin?" the girl asked herself and then she knew.

"All things begin in the white sands of the desert. As the desert seeks the rain, and the sands absorb our tears, so the stories of our lives drift in the winds of those barren lands.

"I was born to the north of our capital in the deserted plains that were the home of many nomadic people before the impending tragic end of our tranquil time marked an exodus towards the captivating civilisation of our cities. My childhood began with colourful silk tents, amidst undulating dunes, besides clear water oases, that then became a journey to the *Revenant Sea,* where, as you know, my father founded a successful fishing business, in the calm eastern waters he found there.

"But be in no doubt, it is the desert that formed my soul. There is nowhere to hide from the fury of its grasp, yet there is nowhere else I would rather be when it opens its heart to offer the gift of its beauty in response to the first touch of moisture. The plants of the desert are a constant sign of hope; the flowers of the desert are a mystery we cannot fathom; the fortitude of the creatures that make the desert their home amazes us all. If you honour and respect the desert it will welcome you - only those who take it for granted or who do not accommodate their lives to it are in danger of its lethal touch.

"In the desert, our people learnt restraint. In its heat, we learnt the foolishness and wastefulness of anger. As we crossed its mountainous sands, we learnt how insubstantial and transitory our treasured possessions really are. In traversing the dunes, we learnt abstinence.

"In burying those who strayed from the path, we learnt that in mutual companionship, we would be saved, and thus we ensured that we never journeyed alone. In the duty of tending the fire, we learnt the heartening task of telling stories that has become our people's greatest achievement. In the prisms of sun light formed by the wind tossed sands, we saw out first mirages and learnt to dream and to fantasise. As we stumbled across our first barren river bed, we gained the spirit to persevere and the strength of endurance to continue against all adversity.

"Yes, my friend, all that is noble purpose for those who dwell on Mnesis has its origins in the desert. It was the stumbling start for our people as we made our first tentative advances towards the civilised world we now see around us. And it was my own beginning when my faltering footsteps as a child turned to self-confidence through tending the camp fire, and finally I gained wisdom enough to know the desert paths coupled with the strength to survive its unbearable heat.

"The sands of the desert are its greatest wonder. We think of them in our ignorance as bland, a constant white presence, an irritation that brings rare waters to dried eyes, that clogs our throats and nostrils. Those sands, however sing to us and they **travel** ... they cross our world to bring precious grains as the memento of far flung lands, no longer white dust but grey and red, yellow and orange, even purple, crimson and green. Those sands that swirl in their maelstroms around us are part of the bounty that is Mnesis, where everything has a purpose and a meaning, just waiting for us to observe and discover it.

"To flee before the sands? To stand in their storm? Or to follow their path? These are the questions that all who dwell in the desert eventually ask. When I found myself asking the same, the choice I made was simple: I chose to be tossed wherever those sands would take me, giving myself in utter faithfulness to the puissance and sustenance of their Composer. I would journey wherever I was taken, no purpose of my own, only his or hers."

Ptere'an could not stop himself interrupting at Shaa'shesh's open admission of her belief in a Creator:

"Your belief in the old concept of the Divine. Does this come from your being in constant danger in the desert? Is it a defence mechanism or a means to provide comfort and consolation for a mind challenged by the risks you faced in your childhood?"

Shaa'shesh grinned. Not at all upset at the interruption. Indeed, she had long learnt that if she was not interrupted, then her constant flow of chatter would ensure no-one else ever got a chance to speak. Being a generous soul, she recognised that others would want to say something every now and again, and so was always gracious if her friends stopped her mid-sentence and was quite happy to concede *a small part* of any conversation to her companions. There was no hope of her being silenced by an interruption and she had never sulked in her life as this wasted valuable talking time.

"I have no words to persuade you that there is a Composer of all we see, nor do I derive comfort from the challenges that my belief in such an entity brings. There is no logic to my belief. No proof. Indeed most proofs would suggest that my belief is falsely held. Am I reassured in myself that there is a God? Not at all! But I enjoy the conversations we have."

"It is all delusion then," Ptere'an muttered sadly. "I had hoped that you at least might have the knowledge of this answer."

"The Master no doubt can show you proofs and use words to convince you of the Composer's reality. I am of much simpler stock. I have faith for one reason: I am happier in a world divinely structured than I would be without his or her guidance. For, when all is said and done, I have the intellect of a butterfly. I am attracted to light ... for no reason I can understand. It is the same with the Divine."

At that Ptere'an had to smile. Shaa'shesh's description of herself demeaned her considerable intelligence, yet he had to admit that her flashes of brilliance and surprising insights were as predictable as the fluttering flight of any butterfly.

"My story from the moment my father chose the swell of the seas in preference to the sands of the land has already been told by me before, I think. You know of the end of the aquarium business, of my father's death, of my becoming fostered to Luca, where I was propositioned by him and forced to flee one storm-tossed night and thus arrive alone to face a new terror in the crowded streets of our capital. I was twelve when I arrived in *Persepolis* and had never seen so many people in one place before.

"To my surprise, instead of feeling overwhelmed by my surroundings, I felt lonely for the first time in my life. I was over-looked, ignored, regarded as below conspicion or as beneath the attention of my peers. I encountered a new thing: status. The order of things within the capital was such that each person I encountered knew their standing and rigidly stuck to it to avoid offence. Whereas, I had no position or place in my new society and thus I could neither be ascribed or described.

"I found that I was close to tears at this wall of silence that greeted me, an invisible cloud of misery that would have drowned me, if I had not done as I always do when feeling lonely. I decided to sing.

"The song I chose was one of my favourites; one that had granted me solace in perilous pass, its charm was to recall the fresh waters of a spring I had found once when long leagues from my tent and in great thirst: simple words and a gay tune. Into the relentless silence of those whose lives were pinioned by position, my song was the pebble that created the ripple that became the wave that washed the river banks clean of all clutter of class.

"People stopped to listen. Feet began to tap in keeping with the gentle beat. Fingers followed pretend keyboards in keeping with my softly sung cadenzas. Heads began to nod. I watched and then held my hand out to a young man, his suit denoting he was an executive of great authority, and I asked him to dance with me. He was too shocked to say "nay" and then too enthralled to consider walking on.

In no time at all, a once sombre marble-floored courtyard had become a place for joyful music, whilst my dancing companion and I enjoyed the refreshing delights of its solitary water feature, to splash in a wild flamenco that would later take some explaining when he arrived on that hot summer's day, in his immaculate silk suit, soaked from head to toe ... but smiling with fond memory.

"Every day after, I was asked to dance and sing as the people of *Persepolis* gradually released themselves from the caged aura of their isolation. I was offered money, but asked for food and shelter instead.

They were bemused at first, but soon the wisest amongst them began to reflect on how happier I seemed when I danced and sang, was fed and sheltered and yet remained un-burdened by possessions. The first of the Master's disciples joined me as friends, to dance and sing with me, to demonstrate that life could be fulfilled without standing or status. We were homeless yet happy.

"Thus, I began to comprehend and complete the calling of the *Founder*. Soon, we were enough to justify a building to ourselves, a gift from the executive I had met on that first frightening day in the capital. He would join us a year later as one of our most diligent of followers. His name was T'mas; in life he was so full of confidence and pride in the choice he had made to become a disciple, always the first to volunteer for the hardest of tasks. But alas he died in the early rush and onslaught of this plague. He was the first of so many for whom I now feel the pain of mourning yet the joy of knowing they must have found a place in paradise for their unselfish service here on Mnesis.

"I was just thirteen when the news came that our planet faced destruction from the aberrant path of a solitary asteroid, spiralling out of control from its former orbit of another planet; a meteor had crashed into the heart of its one-time host, sending it on a new path towards our annihilation.

"I was just fourteen when the Master was elected out of the five thousand Lectors to become the *Determinator of our collective fate*.

Too young to vote, but caring very much about the man whom I had been foretold that I would aid one day, I climbed the highest tree in the capital, a blue *Feltrock* of gigantic proportions, to watch out for him every day. Foolish child that I was ..."

Shaa'shesh ignored the implication of Ptere'an's raised eyebrows and slight smile as he pondered that nothing had changed much there then!

"... for of course the Master found me.

"He stood beneath my tree as I slept and threw a twig at me to wake me up. Needless to say I came crashing down to land sprawling at his feet, but he was neither worried nor offended. Merely bent and helped me up then said to me:

"You have something to tell me."

"I looked into his eyes and saw such sadness there that my own heart jolted in my breast. I remember to this day thinking that the burden of his office and the task to which he had been appointed were clearly too much for this simple yet kind man. So, I said the first thing that came into my head: "Master, if you will climb this tree with me, all will seem possible from the height of its many branches".

"He shook his head, but a gleam of humour now shone in his eyes, causing wrinkles to appear at the corner of each, laughter lines bearing light-heartedness where before his brow had shown stern sorrow. "I have scaled such heights you could not imagine" was his cryptic response. "You have a message for me, my child?"

"At this I had frowned in concentrated effort trying to recall my meeting with the Founder upon the strands before the *Turbulent Turbot*. Something he had said then was important now.

"It was no good! I have the memory of an unwoven net, the recall of a handful of sand. I gave up with my head and let my heart speak instead: "You have the answer to all questions. You must believe in yourself ... but my friends and I can help you."

"The Master blinked. This clearly was not what he had expected to hear at all. He shook his head briefly at my words and then grinned: "I do believe you have forgotten what the Founder told you?" he asked of me and then began to laugh. "Yet it is true that I know what our people must do in the face of the disaster that is to befall us. It is also true that your assistance would be most welcome. Can you do as you are told?"

"I had so wanted to nod my head at this but my innate honesty made me gulp then admit to him: "Not really! I have this tendency to do my own thing without thinking."

"Yet that seemed to please him the most for suddenly his back seemed to straighten as if a great load had been released, he looked steadfastly into the heavens as if giving praise for some blessing, then he held his arms out wide as if seeking to comfort the whole world in his embrace, before turning once more to me to say: "You can let me do the thinking. But to do "our own thing" is precisely what is needed now if we are to have a future."

"We talked for hours it seemed after that, although to be fair it could not have been longer than an hour at most, as dusk soon drew in and when the stars lit above me, I became distracted by their many stories. The Master watched my awe and adoration at their brilliance, never diminishing even though I regarded their stellar display every night for years without fail, and thus the Founder's intent was achieved:

"It was never the Founder's words that you were to give me this day," I recall the Master whispering. "You have renewed my strength of purpose through seeing **your wonder at creation** ... that is the Founder's gift for me out of this, our meeting. Please, Shaa'shesh, will you be my aid? My name is Sala'am."

"Again, my story from here is well-known to you. For the last four years, I have followed our Master faithfully. My friends became his disciples, helping spread his message of hope and enabling the *story feste* that is his gift to our departing world to become a reality.

"Thus, we protect the Master as he deliberates on a final solution to the conundrum we set him on taking office. I am convinced that he has a solution, yet even I, whom perhaps am closest to him save one other person, do not know what that solution might be."

Ptere'an's head went up sharply in surprise at the girl's last words and he could not stop himself asking in genuine astonishment:

"Someone knows the Master better than you?"

"If you seek to know the Master, whilst he will always share his heart with me, there is only one person who understands the Master's intent. You have met him already. A great scientist and one whose discovery is at the centre of all that the Master seeks to contrive."

Ptere'an would dearly have liked to question the girl further. Indeed, he was sorely tempted to strangle her for being so cryptic, but their conversation was interrupted by the return of one of the medical attendants, who had brought a mask in for Ptere'an to wear:

"I do not understand why you are not wearing this?" the carer admonished him in some anxiety. "Although Shaa'shesh is not contagious herself, any of the staff here could be carrying the lethal virus that has decimated our people, and you cannot assume that you are protected in any way, just because through chance you have yet to contract the contagion."

"Forgive me," Ptere'an replied and held out his hand for the mask that she offered, then paused in thought, before continuing ruminatively: “I have been tested as has my wife, and neither of us have anything approaching an antivirus to protect us, and yet we have both survived contact with my daughter for many months. M’tew is likewise seemingly immune to the disease. The health of Za’astra, my own daughter, is improving, despite having had the plague for months when most succumb in days … she also has been tested and nothing found out of the ordinary in her serum to explain this.”

Then turning to Shaa’shesh, he asked in hope: “What have your own blood tests revealed?”

“Absolutely nothing,” the girl replied. “For one, I have the disease so no-one has really bothered but, second, I cannot stand needles so I refused to be tested!”

“Pardon!” gasped Ptere’an stunned at this revelation and then he turned to the carer who was nodding in resigned agreement as she muttered: “Shaa’shesh really is the worst patient we have ever had and notoriously stubborn when she wants to be!”

“She is also the one thing that my family and the young man M’tew have in common and we all appear to have developed some possible immunity to the plague that faces our world, so I strongly suggest you ignore this girl’s squeamishness when faced with a needle and start testing her for whatever it is in her blood that appears to have saved my life and the lives of those I hold dear.”

Shaa’shesh gasped but shook her head vigorously before saying:

“Please do not! I really, really, do not like needles.”

“Think of M’tew,” Ptere’an admonished her. “You could save his life or at least save him from a slow and painful death,” which silenced the girl sufficiently to allow her to recover her courage and then to nod her acquiescence to the attendant.

“There is no pain and it only takes a few seconds,” the girl’s carer reassured her with the traditional well-intentioned lie. “We will have the results of the tests in seconds and you can watch the display screen to your left for the analysis. Best you look away as the needles go in, if you are not accustomed to them.”

A small compartment in Shaa’shesh’s bedstead opened to release a robotic arm which moved forwards silently to hold the girl’s left wrist in its irresistible grasp whilst it did a topographic scan for a suitable vein. Then there was the sound of the spray of local anaesthetic and disinfectant being administered, a sharp and sudden prick of a needle, the release of blood into built-in receptacles concealed within the robotic arm, before the whole contraption began to slowly return to its home behind the girl's head.

The procedure had taken barely a few seconds. Shaa'shesh, however, had fainted the moment the needle had hit one of her veins and was now lying out cold on her bed, much to Ptere'an's surprise, as he had seen the girl withstand much greater pain before and do so stoically.

"She really does not like needles," acknowledged the attendant "but at least we have found a way of making her be quiet and go to sleep!"

A chime sounded to indicate the test results were ready to be reviewed on the bedside monitor and they both turned to read the long message displayed there:

Patient: **Shaa'shesh**
Admitted: 04/13/4511

Preliminary diagnosis:
Patient has unresponsive viral contagion (S112).
Early signs of respiratory damage
Liver function at 94%
Heart disease with heart performance reduced to 88%
Patient is in third stage of contagion (there are four stages, the fourth is fatal in 100% of cases)

Symptoms:
Fever
Cellular breakdown in epidermis consistent with second and third stages of contagion
Discoloration and swelling of tongue and feet, consistent with second stage of contagion
Anaemia
Lethargy
Heart performance reduced by 12% indicating at least one silent heart event and indication of movement to fourth stage of disease
Above is usually preliminary to massive heart and respiratory failure, marking onset of fourth and fatal stage of contagion.
Initial prognosis: less than 1% chance of survival. Death predicted within four days.

Last reported state:
Unresponsive to antibiotics. Respiratory system: stable. Liver performance: stable at 94%. Kidney performance: potassium levels low, calcium levels high, no indication of long term damage. Heart permanently damaged but stable. Other organ performance: in normal range and stable.

Revised diagnosis: Patient remains temporarily arrested in third stage of contagion (S112).

Results of blood analysis:
Patient has Type 7 blood (in common with 3% of population), white cell count at -12%, potassium abnormally low (62% compared to the population norm), calcium remains high (134% compared to population norm), otherwise other counts are in the normal range, except for unusually high presence of unique enzyme that is functioning as a meta-biotic. Some indication that the meta-biotic is inducing a slight but important change in subject's DNA, providing the basis for genetic protection against the unknown virus that is attacking her system.

Analysis of meta-biotic:
Elemental composition chart is displayed in top right hand corner of the screen. Layered bonding observed and thus easy to break down into component parts, although lateral bonds are covalent. Similar in structure to common addition polymers, but containing two rare elements not found on this planet, one of which is in column 28 and row 7 on the periodic table with zero Mass to high Energy relationship (theonic) and atomic structure off previously known scale but including intronic ability.

There is no known source on our planet for these two rare elements which the subject is producing as part of an enzyme from the periotic and seri-aortic glands in the neurological and lower gastro intestinal regions. The impact of the enzyme appears to be two-fold: first it is interrupting the life cycle of the viral contagion such that the viral spread is in arrest and progression to the fourth stage seems unlikely. Second, it has already modified the subject's DNA such that further risk of contagion appears to be less than 1%

No certainty this will prevent the viral contagion from having already permanently and fatally harmed the subject but probability of using subject's DNA to create immunity in those yet to contract disease is analysed as 98% chance of success.

Revised prognosis:
No indication of further progression to fourth stage of contagion. Viral spread has ceased and early indication is that the life cycle of the virus is being permanently interrupted by meta-biotics being self-produced within subject's serum. 41% chance of survival depending on damage to organs thus far. Principle risk is state and speed of recovery from minor liver and heart damage.

"What does it mean?" Ptere'an asked the carer, but she could not answer, as with tears in her eyes, she switched on the inter-communicator to speak tremulously to her immediate superior, saying simply: "We have our cure for the plague!"

In the days that followed, Shaa'shesh had to endure being injected by *a lot* of needles, as the geneticists of her planet made use of her serum to mass-produce the inoculations needed to save a previously doomed people. Shaa'shesh herself began to recover, as her liver stabilised and the contagion receded; she did not, however, lose her phobia of needles and after passing out several times, her carers decided it was best to keep her permanently asleep ... and so she dreamt of flying trees and singing stars, whilst the rest of the hospital had peace from her chatter and mischief at last.

As she slept, M'tew and Ptere'an took it in turns to keep her company, both holding her frail hands to comfort her, but now in hope, whilst proudly contemplating the simple girl whose blood was to be the source of life for a whole planet.

On day five after Ptere'an's discovery of the cure for the plague, Za'astra came to visit the sleeping Shaa'shesh. Her life had been saved by the kiss she had shared with the young disciple, and in turn that kiss had revealed the previously unknown potency of Shaa'shesh's blood, for had the disciple not contracted the contagion, then her world would never have discovered the secret of their long-term immunity to the plague.

In her childlike innocence, Za'astra believed that this had been pre-ordained, and as soon as she had received her inoculation and recovered sufficiently to leave her bedroom and the gardens in which she played with her father, she came to give praise and thanks to the friend she now loved as much as her own family. Thus it was that Za'astra, in the fullness of health herself, a state that Shaa'shesh had never seen her in before, was the first person to greet the girl as she woke finally from her drug-induced sleep to look at a world no longer threatened by the creeping and invisible devastation of disease.

"I scarcely recognised you," Shaa'sehsh whispered through parched lips as she glanced at her friend from the lowered eye lashes of tired eyes. Za'astra gasped to hear her friend speak, then bent forward and kissed her on the lips, on her eyes, her hands and her hair with total abandonment, such was her great joy at the return of the disciple to consciousness, before exclaiming loudly for all to hear:

"The world rejoices, the seas are stilled, the winds draw breath, the heavens alight, the future is bright, fear departs at your delight, my dearest."

"Well I am happy to see you too" Shaa'shesh replied, a little overwhelmed by this welcome, but then she could not stop herself and began to chuckle. "Is everyone going to be this happy to see me awake? I must confess, I do not merit this ... but I fully intend to lap up every moment of it. A bit of adulation never did anyone any harm in my view, deserved or otherwise!"

"You have saved all of our lives," Za'astra reminded her, "So you had better get used to the odd word of praise or two. As for me, I am just happy you are awake. I always knew you would save me anyway. I prayed for this after all. But enough talking, I am here to get you out of bed. There is someone who definitely wants to see you and I am to take you to him."

M’tew was standing shyly on the glazed balcony that opened out from Shaa’shesh’s private room at the Medical Centre and looked down over the Forum with its twin rows of stately Plane trees. He held her hand briefly, tentatively, frightened that he might lose her again, as he almost had already to the ravages of plague, just scarce days before. But she would have none of his reticence, and brushing aside his gentle touch, grasped him firmly around his neck, pulled his head down to meet hers, and kissed him with unrestrained passion on the lips. When finally both came up for air, she laughingly teased him:

“I could hardly do that with a swollen tongue covered in purple and green spots, now, could I?”

“I would not have minded,” replied her lover, “Yet I am glad you are well and that we can spend these last two days in each other’s company. The end of our world means so little to me to know that I can live it with you.”

“Hush, my love, for the next few days are the beginning and not the end. We shall live forever in love, and these two days are a foretaste of an eternity of that love.”

But M’tew shook his head at her words: “How can you still believe? And how can I learn of eternal love in such a short time? If there is a Creator, surely he can come up with something better than this end for us? Some extension of the time allotted such that you and I can have an example of love to take into the next life, if such truly exists?”

Shaa’shesh smiled and replied to his doubts without hesitation:

“When compared with the vastness that is the Divine Creation, we are mere particles of dust, no more, blown upon the raging tempest of the ravaging winds of unrepentant time. Yet to be mere dust blown by solar flares to visit the wonders of our Universe is such an awesome thing to hope for. To see the stars, to drift from the outer atmosphere of one planet to the next – how wonderful is that?

“There is so little of that time left, my love. Surely we can spend it wisely and well, without either rancour or argument, just enjoying the beauty of our surroundings and the delight of each other’s company? Can we not make our end simple in this way? Must we look for more than we have been given? For I am content with one second in your company yet am offered *two whole days*!”

At that M'tew could not stop himself but began to laugh. At first it was a melancholy sound, but as he recalled her sense of childlike glee as Shaa'shesh had said "two whole days", his laugh became a guffaw that shook him from head to toe, whilst the girl hugged him with pride for the return of his good humour. When finally, M'tew's habitual seriousness had returned, the odd twitch at the corner of his mouth the only sign that the laughter was still rebounding within him, Shaa'shesh gave his hand a quick squeeze and then said:

"Take me to my trees. It is no good us standing up here looking down at them. I need to talk to them ... well climb at least one anyway."

As they stood together, looking out across the stone terraces of their capital towards the avenue of trees that edged their world's most ancient meeting place, the *Forum of Paraclemos*, Shaa'shesh sighed at the majesty of the ancient arbours which had stood sentinel over this place of quiet reflection and congregation for several hundreds of years. Her quiet reflection was abruptly disturbed, however, by the first of the meteor strikes that were the presage of the last days of her world and the announcement of the unwelcome arrival of the asteroid.

The first of the fire-stones crashed through the Plane tree before her, which shuddered briefly and then was engulfed in a pillar of white heat. Shaa'shesh screamed, before running towards the remaining trees, whilst M'tew stood horrified at the terrible risk the girl was taking:

"You fool," he shouted after her, "The trees are not worth it. Come back! We must find the shelters."

Around him, the people of Mnesis were already heading for the municipal subterranean shelters that had been built in preparation for this terrifying pass beneath the great public buildings of the capital. Every square and piazza had been prepared with tunnels delving deep within the rocky foundations of the mountain on which the capital perched. Hundreds of thousands could be housed in comfort within the brightly-lit labyrinthine corridors hidden beneath the city. Every inhabitant of *Paraclemos* knew what they must do as the klaxon went off to warn them of the first destructive descent of the asteroid. Every inhabitant, *save one*, ran towards the nearest shelter entrance.

The flames of burning trees swirled around Shaa'shesh but she ignored their intense heat and plunged deeper and deeper into danger to emerge carrying a small and frightened child from the centre of the fiery maelstrom, and then ran back to join M'tew where he stood dumbfounded.

As she approached him, she handed him the child then said:

"You thought I wished to save the trees?"

M'tew nodded.

"Then I must teach you to have *faith*."

Once more, the girl stepped out into the meteoric fires, which lapped around her but left her miraculously untouched. The intensity of the heat was such that M'tew was forced to cover his face ... but he could not look away from the sight of his beautiful love, striding towards the desecrated remnants of her once proud Plane trees, intent on her own self immolation in the flames of their destruction, committing suicide for an ideal and a set of beliefs he did not understand and could not share with her.

He watched as she stood defying the conflagration that tried to engulf her, and then she held out her hands in humble supplication. For a moment, the flames died back, but their ferocity returned with new vigour, and, in tears, Shaa'shesh fled their terrible grasp to run into M'tew's waiting arms and then follow him to the safety of the tunnels below.

Yet in the brief moment, when the fury of the fires had been restrained, the scientists watching the path of the asteroid in their tracking stations in the *Space Port of Melchor* detected a pause in its persistent journey towards Mnesis - an unexplained delay in its descent, a temporary halt in its previously uninterrupted progression towards the demolition of their planet. As one they turned towards Sala'am, quietly contemplating the same on his personal monitor, and cheered. For this moment had been predicted.

"It is too late to save our planet," the Master reminded them. "It has taken the immediate threat of impending planetary destruction to boost the intellect of just one of our disciples to the elevated point where we can tap into the powers of nature and turn them upon themselves. Yet Mnesis requires many hundreds of our people to be so similarly inspired if we would seek to turn the asteroid above us from its intended path of destruction. Sadly, we have only one Shaa'shesh, and her fellow disciples are already perished, but her example of what we can become will aid those who are destined to follow us."

M'tew clung to his distraught souls mate, hoping beyond all hope that the ache in his heart from the love and pride he felt for Shaa'shesh would communicate itself through the veil of her innumerable tears that briefly separated them. She had saved a child at risk of her own life, then tried to save a whole world, an act beyond all reason and comprehension, yet impossibly made feasible for the briefest of instances, just to prove to him that she had *faith*. His attempts at solace were rebuffed by the walls of her solitude and so he tried dark humour:

"Your tears would wash any meteor storm away, my love."

"Oh!" she gasped, "You ... you ... wonderful man" and her laughter returned as she wiped her eyes and blew her nose to shake away the sad memories of the loss of her beloved Plane trees.

Then Shaa'shesh looked around to take in her surroundings and saw the look on the faces of her people. Pride was there in their eyes, at what they had all been honoured briefly to perceive. The whole world had seen her act of defiance and its momentary impact. They had also seen her fail ... yet hope lingered. Hope tempered with something else, however.

"I am truly apart," the girl whispered to M'tew and he nodded sadly in agreement. "I still love you. But yes, you are become something we do not understand."

She looked up at him, then. Now she was bewildered that he also should think her different just because of a single act that had been divinely-aided and was none of her doing. She did not know what to say that would change his perception of her. This was all too new for her, too recently happened for her to fully comprehend, too upsetting for her sense of reason to find a response.

"I have not changed and my love for you will never change" was all she could think of to say, yet knew it was not nearly enough to fill the growing chasm between herself and those around her. Nor did her words comfort the man holding her, who released her from his embrace, then shrugged before saying:

"I am in no doubt of your love for me. But how can you say you are one of us, when you talk to animals and trees, know our most intimate thoughts and thus can resolve our daily problems, and have the power to control the path of an asteroid or resist the fury of a meteorite?"

Shaa'shesh knelt at his feet in tears once more and looking up into his eyes, pleaded with him for his understanding:

"Not mine but HIS will was done. Not me but divinely have these things been accomplished. Not I but in God's hands and through his grace has all that you have seen come to pass."

He was, however, beyond convincing and shaking his head at both her deference and denial of difference, broke her delicate heart with his parting words:

"I return to the love of my family. They I understand. I wish you well and, who knows, if your vision of a life after this is true, then maybe you can find me there? But I would be with those who are of my own kind. It is possible, I have heard, to love each other yet not be suited to live together. That alas is how I see it that we have become."

At which he walked away from her and into the crowds in the subway where they had taken shelter, soon disappearing from her hazy view, as the last of her tears dried in grey streaks upon her discoloured cheeks. She stood unsteadily, blinded in her misery, and staggered for an exit, trying to flee in shame from the multitudes looking on at her sadly, yet also showing their respect for M'tew's decision. Those gathered around her helped her shaking hands to find the rails of the staircase that led to the apartments above ground. None knew if the buildings above had survived the first devastating strikes from the asteroid, but all understood Shaa'shesh's desire to be alone at this moment.

Shaa'shesh reached the ground floor and walked through the glass atrium of the towering office complex above the shelter where she and M'tew had only moments before shared their sad parting. She looked around her and saw that she was alone. Then she knelt once more and looking towards the apex of the building and the solar flares of a gathering dusk, absorbed the first glimmering of the evening stars, before asking:

"Forgive me, lord, for I have erred yet do not know what it is that I have done wrong. Surely it cannot be right that I have forced my lover away when he needs my comfort and support? Give me the inspiration to perceive your will in this and let me follow your path."

Some hours later, in darkness save for the shallow light of a distant Old Moon, she was still kneeling in silent prayer, conversing with the Universal Being, when the Master finally found her. He did not kneel, merely waited in silence besides her until she acknowledged his presence with a shrug of her shoulders and a gruff "harrumph", before standing to greet him with a shy hug and a half-hearted, part-humorous, part self-deprecating question:

"You don't think I am become different do you?"

"We are all different hence the importance we give to tolerance and respect. *Remember* Nar'csa and the greater love her parents felt for her because of her uniqueness. *Remember* LeCerf, who stands alone yet is part of the herd. *Remember* Bart'l'mew whose friendship crossed the boundaries of his lost senses. *Remember* the uniqueness of Orama's tent or Numa'mesh's potatoes or Wassail's rhubarb ale. *Remember* that Luca loved both of his sons, but did so differently. *Remember* the shoals of fish and the crowds of former fishermen who came to rescue you at the *Turbulent Turbot*. *Remember* the innocent comfort of Perditus, the courage of Za'astra's daily prayer or Shemer's surprising sacrifice. There is no single way to show our love for each other - rather we all find our own special way to do so."

"Then why am I alone?"

"M'tew needed to show his unselfish love just as you had done when you tried to save the world with your act of faith. He realised he could not save you ... or rather there was nothing he could do to save you that you could not do yourself. So he has gone to offer his comfort and strength to his family who need it more than you do, even though his heart remains here."

"I need him too!" cried the girl near desperation.

"No, you do not," replied the Master calmly. "You have a task to do and M'tew would have prevented it if he were here."

"Oh! Does *the Path* have to be so complicated? M'tew's leaving was pre-ordained then?"

The Master laughed at this. He had often reflected that the simplicity of Shaa'shesh's faith was part of her charm. Her absolute belief in the Composer's power to pull the strings of every aspect of her life made her an ideal servant to his will. Yet Divine Will was not like that at all: opportunities to do good would arise and these would be grasped, but the Composer was as interested in the extemporaneous as in the pre-ordained; in variations around a theme as in the precision of composition; in seeking sympathy as much as symphony.

"My dear, God merely takes advantage of this chance, no more. Had you and M'tew not separated, another way would have been found. Have faith."

The flames of the firestorm that had destroyed the avenue of trees in the *Forum* had long died down as Shaa'shesh and Sala'am walked beneath the stars, and spoke of their hopes and ambitions for the end of all songs. This was to be the last dance of their people, who lived in harmony with their world's spirit, whose gift to the universal path was to leave a memory of grace under pressure, and an example of the power of evolution when moulded in unity with faith to face the stress of adversity.

The disciple had assumed their immediate destination was to have been the *Bibliotechnaoi*, for no other reason than that the Master's First Address still bound them both to its promise of redemption, so she was surprised to find herself back at the deserted Medical Centre. Seeing her frown in question, the Master smiled reassuringly before saying:

"It is time you learnt what I have been doing for the last four years. You, more than anyone, have bought me the time I needed to do what had to be done. I owe it to you that you see this. So, I am giving you access to my secret files on our planetary server. But to do this I need you to be in private and with access to a computer monitor. Your room here at the Medical Centre seemed to me to be the best place where I can give you the privacy you need to read my records without disturbance."

Shaa'shesh nodded in wonder, her childlike curiosity aroused in full, her generous heart warming to the gift of confidence that the Master was showing in her. Together, they arrived at the room where only hours before she had woken to the joy of Za'astra's greeting, and she sat on the bed, turning to the bedside monitor to log on.

The Master bent over her left shoulder and typed in his access codes to open up a series of files for the girl to read:

"**Omega Project. Access restricted.**" she read with growing interest, and so engrossed did she become in the account before her that she did not notice the Master silently leave the room.

The first files were accounts of the successful experiments at *Melchor* in the development of cryogenics. The advances were such that they promised the ability to sustain life for a billion years. They finished however with the Master's short and simple evaluation: *"Three billion too short"*

Next she read of the development of great space ships: Stellar Arks that could traverse over hundreds of light years distance in the ten thousand years of velocity their powerful engines could guarantee space flight.

"Insufficient to find a life giving alternative" the Master had written sadly, *"and only 1% of our people would survive. Would our collective psyche survive the knowledge that we had sacrificed 99% of our people to save 1%? Would we be marked forever with shame? Or face a lonely death in the cold of the vacuum of space?"*

The third folder contained a set of files about the predicted changes in the people of her world of Mnesis, as the impending crisis of their collective destruction became ever more imminent. She read of the development of new emotions and behaviours forecast by the top psychologists of her world:

Behaviour Changes. Summary

Without a distracting purpose or some noble combining intent, we anticipate any and all of the following: incidences of harm done by one citizen to another; emotions of stress resulting in the raising of blood pressure and the temporary loss of reason; tricks being played on people with the intention of harm and ridicule rather than fun; an increase in materiality, excessive social activity, even excesses of eating and drinking of alcohol; increasing isolation often accompanied by over-reliance on the distraction of alcohol or narcotics; tendencies to self destruction, possibly even self-mutilation and most worryingly suicide.

On the positive side, we also forecast the same stresses will result in elevated mental abilities amongst those with the highest intellect and most inspired to save or protect our world. We identify a particular classification of individual most likely to make the next evolutionary break-through: those unbound by belief in science, most open to the fantastical, closest to and most desirous to be one with the natural, separated from any concept of materiality, and young enough to be open to new thought patterns and concepts. We cannot be certain how this next evolutionary step will present itself but it may provide a means to save our planet.

Beneath this, the Master had written his own evaluation: *I am blessed with my disciples but will they evolve in time to aid us? As to the terrible prospect that my people lose their touching grace, I must find them a "noble combining intent" to prevent the new emotions from ever being born.*

The fourth folder was marked: **The Solution**. She opened this hungrily and was totally surprised to see that the files included a short paper from Numa'mesh's husband, J'hon. It began succinctly:

Introducing Introns. *J'hon, Reproductive and Genetics Programme Director*
This tract summarises my discovery on **Introns**, a type of RNA that is essential to our whole concept of life. Introns are the triggers that induce the combination of RNA to form DNA molecules. My studies indicate that without their presence, this replication cannot proceed. My studies also identify

the conditions in which Introns will react with RNA - these conditions are important as there are specific parameters of both pressure (>0.05a, <32a and heat >-75Ke <735Ke) within which Introns will and will not survive, whilst both carbon and oxygen are required in their evolved forms (and not as part of air borne polymers or as methane).

It is well-known that the combination of RNA to form the molecular double helix spirals of DNA sits at the root of the development of life and, in particular, the continued evolution and genetic inheritance that is at the heart of life-forms passing down their inheritance to successor life forms beyond death. However, the trigger for such combination does not appear within the DNA or RNA which we have studied. Or rather, our studies *until recently* had assumed the trigger for combination sat within every molecule of RNA and that our understanding of RNA combination was faulty. Introns are so rare that their identification has eluded us for centuries, until now.

Our most recent discovery is that in less than one trillionth of RNA, there exists a catalytic enzyme or "trigger" that induces the combination of RNA to form DNA. Once the initial combination has been induced the process of combination continues at first as a simple but covalent polymerisation, subsequently developing to additional polymerisation with Introns providing the catalyst to form DNA.

The second file in this folder was a summary of a space probe undertaken on Mnesis' sister planet, Earth, just two years earlier. It was marked, cryptically:

The Ultimate Solution (update)
The current conditions on Earth are not suitable for the combination of RNA to form DNA, being outside the parameters for the survival of Introns (temperature is currently over 2400Ke and predicted to remain above 750Ke for approximately 750,000 Earth rotations or 670,000 Mnemonic years).

750,000 rotations is still within the time parameters set by the Master. More disturbing is the absence of the enzyme that is essential to the function of Introns, with no evidence of Introns within the RNA community analysed.

Conclusion: Introns do not exist on Earth due to its slower pace of evolution. There is no potential for sentient life or evolution therefore on the Planet Earth

Beneath this report, the Master had written two comments:

"Thus ends our hope of noble sacrifice" followed by a subsequent reflection: *"Unless another source of Introns can be found."*

The third and final file in this folder was entitled **The Genome Project.** Once more it began with a simple summary, this time by Gilga'mell, the chief medical officer.

Update on the Genome Project

Professor Gilga'mell, chief medical officer, Mnesis
This project was originally funded as academic research to examine the prognosis that there are a finite set of combinations of DNA within the inherited molecular structures of the people of Mnesis.

This would in turn form the baseline for further applied research into re-engineering our genetic profile to accelerate evolution or to repress inherited disabling conditions and diseases, whilst also opening up the possibility of cloning healthy cells, organs and even our people.

Four years ago, the project was set a new goal by our elected Master: the capture of the RNA and DNA structures of every citizen in Mnesis to be kept in suspended cryogenic storage.

I can report that we have achieved the target of 100% population capture but will continue to keep the programme open for new births until day 0.

Regrettably, I have to report that early indications are that the genetic material we have collected is already infected with the viral strain (S112) that is currently decimating our population. It is unlikely that any DNA produced from this material would survive and more likely that if we introduce our RNA and DNA into any new environment, we would also introduce the virus into the same environment, further reducing the likelihood of sentient life evolving.

The fifth folder came as a complete shock to her as it was a series of communications with someone she knew all too well:

Message to the Master from the Founder
I have Found Her

Congratulations on your election.

We have not met nor are likely to, but I have been working on a project that may assist you in developing your solution to the crisis that our race currently faces. I would prefer to remain anonymous, and so have chosen a pseudo-name that reflects the important discovery I have made. Please refer to me as the Founder ("Found Her") in any correspondence from now.

My work involves testing individuals of high intellect for potentially latent mental powers. It is fair to say that to date my work has been unsuccessful, but the purpose of this message is to tell you that I have found an ideal subject, and one whom already has shown signs of the empathy that is the precursor to clairvoyance and telepathy.

Why should this interest you?

If my forecasts are correct, the impending catastrophe that we face will trigger a new stage of our racial evolution. It may even see this progress to the point where some of our race will go on to develop both creativity and telekinesis, sufficient to protect us from the destruction of the asteroid that approaches us.

I shall watch the subject carefully and my intention is to test her once I see the signs of telepathy that mark the first step of her evolution. More important, I predict that her existing high levels of empathy will encourage her to mix with those who have the same potential for evolution to greater powers as she does. So I advise that you watch out for those with whom she associates or befriends and take them under your wing. They will be invaluable in supporting your own programme for saving our world as well as representing one potential hope for our collective survival.

Message to the Master from the Founder
Today I tested her

I took a huge risk today.

Starting at the beginning: it is clear from recent accounts of the subject's actions that she has developed a high degree of telepathy unwittingly and also is showing some signs of clairvoyance (as predicted).

So today I posed a threat to her life at a time when she was psychologically vulnerable, hoping to induce a boost in her other latent abilities. The results were remarkable. Though unconscious and drowning, her natural defence mechanisms were able to communicate with and command the aid of several shoals of fish, demonstrating not only advanced telepathy but also the ability to control others which is one of the highest brain functions.

Message to the Master from the Founder
I agree with your analysis

Thank you for your message.

I have reviewed the results of the tests that you sent through and conclude that the subject has subconsciously used her latent creative talents to genetically modify her own serum, in order to create the meta-biotic your medical staff have been seeking as the antidote to the plague that threatened our world. We are, therefore, days away from her latent talents evolving to the point where teleportation and telekinesis also become feasible. It will need only one further crisis or threat to our world which she feels the need to respond to in order to shatter the self-imposed boundaries on her talents (a result of her inherent humility and self-doubt).

Beneath this was a single comment from the Master: *"We have lost her disciples and there is only one of her. Too little, too late for us, yet remarkable for those who shall follow us."*

The sixth folder was the progress report on the construction of a new Stellar Ark in the *Space Port of Melchor*.

Project Completion report
Stellar Ark. Evolution
Professor M'rca, Chief Astro-Engineer

The two year programme to construct a stellar transporter that will be able to withstand the intense heat on the surface of the Planet Earth for a period of at least 750,000 Earth rotations has concluded successfully today.

The ship is designed for the specified crew and has cargo capacity for the cryogenic chambers needed to maintain its cargo stored safely for the required period. Shell life and cryogenic storage facilities have both been tested for durability, as far as we are able to do so. These tests have been successful.

The Stellar Ark named *Evolution* represents the height of our protective technology. Its proposed short flight path has meant we have been able to switch power from propulsion to protection and regeneration, giving the on board generators, supplemented by solar panelling, a life in excess of a

billion years, or well within the parameters set by the Master.
To which the Master had added a single comment: *"We are ready then."*

The seventh and final folder was Sala'am's most Recent Document folder. It contained a conversation between Professor Gilga'mell and the Master earlier that day which set Shaa'shesh's heart racing.

Gilga'mell to Sala'am
14/13/4511 18:45
We do not have enough serum to save our people AND reverse the damage done to the genome we have taken.

Sala'am to Gilga'mell
14/13/4511 18:46
What do we need?

Gilga'mell to Sala'am
14/13/4511 18:48
We need more protein from the serum of the surviving subject. But if we take any more of her blood she will die. She is very weak as it is Sala'am to Gilga'mell

Sala'am to Gilga'mell
14/13/4511 18:49
Can we not replicate it?

Gilga'mell to Sala'am
14/13/4511 18:51
Given time, but to go direct to its source is so much quicker? Is this the end of your vision, my friend?

Sala'am to Gilga'mell
23/17/4511 18:52
We carry on. The future of our race is no longer in our hands but in the hands of another (and always has been). Trust me, my brother, we will have nothing to fear.

Shaa'shesh laughed to herself with childlike and unrestrained joy.

"Master, I understand what it is that you seek. Your solution for our future is brilliant and so worthy of our people," she whispered happily to herself. Then turning to the computer console she issued her final instructions in life:

"Reconnect the intravenous link to patient named Shaa'shesh and commence transfusion. Override safety mechanisms (access code: Master 11/1418) and withdraw 100% of subject's blood for immediate transmission to the laboratory of chief medical officer Gilga'mell. Override alarm systems until patient life signs have ceased. Send e-message confirmation to "The Master", actual name Sala'am, with this final message: *Thank you, my friend, for allowing me to make this difference."*

Then she lay back on the hospital bed as the robotic arm swung out from the wall and administered the injection of mild anaesthetic into her left forearm that was the prelude to connecting the silver tubes that would suck the life-blood from her. With the slightest of smiles on her lips, she gradually fell into the long and permanent sleep of blood-loss. Her final whispered words before she passed out were a simple plea: "Let there be trees in paradise."

Thus it was that the eleventh story to go onto the disc that would be the testimonial of the peaceful people of Mnesis was the story of **the sacrifice of one girl's blood** to provide a serum for a people already doomed to death.

When the people of Mnesis heard of Shaa'shesh's death, they looked up at the asteroid that was their nemesis, and suddenly it seemed very close indeed.

Interlude

The Programme Director looked across at Annabelle, the tears still pouring down her cheeks from her re-reading of the last dying moments of Shaa'shesh.

The young scientist had recently joined the programme as an ambitious and enthusiastic student, but with her discovery of the contents of the box, found on Pallas, she had changed. At first she had been absorbed by the stories she had uncovered.

Perhaps she had become too involved in the strange and alien race that had once lived a few million miles from our own planet? For now, a rare sadness, almost remorse, gripped her as if something she treasured had been lost.

The director looked down again onto

the transcript she had given him to read the day before and frowned. He could not see why the stories had taken such a hold on the girl?

A collection of small and insignificant descriptions in an ancient "time capsule" that told them nothing of great note about a race of aliens who had been destroyed over 4 billion years ago. Interesting anthropologically but why the emotional reaction from his colleague? The director decided to challenge her reaction, to see if he could discover the root cause beneath her tears:

"I had hoped for a description of their technology, their advances in science, their knowledge of the geology or the cosmology that surrounded them, some inkling of how they had mastered space travel, even a description of how they looked and reproduced. Laws, politics, wars, conflicts, treaties, histories, plays even – any of this would have helped me understand the people of Mnesis better!

Instead I have a recipe, a description of a child's tent, the story of a father who loved both his sons, someone offering their best beer at a beer festival, a stranger helping another, a surprise catch for a fisherman, someone else who tricked a neighbour, a lost child found, a young girl who prayed in silence, another child spell-bound by a beautiful view, a deaf man who helps a blind man climb a tree, and then another girl who sacrifices her life for a serum for a people who are going to die anyway only a few hours later.

It is not exactly earth-shatteringly newsworthy. I am in no doubt I could find eleven such stories if I went out onto the streets of Cambridge or Boston right now!"

Then noticing Annabelle was glaring back at him, he conceded graciously:

"Alright! I accept these people seem to be universally *'nice'* and *'decent'*. They even appear to be genetically predisposed towards peaceful co-existence in a way that would be wonderful if it were true here on Earth. Anger and violence are obviously not part of their genes, mores, behaviour or creed, and this is laudable. But they are not human. Their genetic make-up is different from ours and I cannot see that their society and actions can teach us very much I am afraid."

Annabelle pushed the last pages of the transcript of the account from Mnesis across her superior's desk.

"You have not read the twelfth story yet. I kept it back as I needed to see how you would react to the other eleven. If it will help, your reaction was the same as mine ... until I read this. But I can now tell you that you are wrong on so many levels. There is no genetic predisposition to peaceful coexistence within the make-up of the people of Mnesis. Ptere'an's assault on Shaa'shesh shows us that.

The people of Mnesis *chose* their way of life and *kept to it* despite the terrible end they faced. This final chapter of their sacrifice for *us*, shows that the choice they made is as relevant to the human race as ever it was to the wonderful people of that dying planet.

The last chapter is the Master's story."

Ptere'an held the precious disc in his hand, a set of eleven stories that best represented the true worth of his people. He should have been overjoyed by his achievement, yet the price of their survival as a people now seemed too great in the wake of Shaa'shesh's departure.

"Master, I know that you asked for twelve stories, but we are all agreed that the memory of Shaa'shesh's blood, given to us as a loving sacrifice that we might all have further life, should mark the end of our account here on Mnesis. There is no other story that could follow the tale of her death."

Sala'am hugged Ptere'an, momentarily speechless with the tears still drying on his own cheeks at the memory of the young disciple's peaceful end. But he knew he could not remain silent. The gift of his people and their accomplishment of the task that he had set them deserved acknowledgement. He inhaled deeply then spoke that all should hear his words:

"Ptere'an. I have said before that I am blessed in you and indeed this is true. You have done all and more than I could ever have hoped. Eleven stories are enough. For the task of telling the last story is mine. I receive the box and the disc on which you have recorded the telling of our lives and shall take it to our Haven at *Melchor*, where a space ship is waiting for me to transport it to Pallas. I do not know if there shall be time for me to return to our planet to be with you at our end, so I bid you farewell now, my brothers and sisters."

His words were greeted with silence. A combination of respect for his last selfless act of delivering the disc and thus condemning himself to a lonely death, mingled with regret that the Master would not be able to join them in the last moments of the world they knew he loved dearly.

They stood in silence watching the monitors in the amphitheatre that had been their home for the duration of the *story feste,* before offering a polite ripple of applause as a single and lonely space ship launched from the Haven and within minutes was circling Pallas.

Then the ship broke orbit.

But instead of returning towards their planet, it used the gravity of Pallas to sling-shot into space, heading away from both the asteroid and Mnesis as the asteroid began its final descent. Rather, the stellar ship *Evolution* headed out into the safety of distant space.

Ptere'an turned towards the bewildered crowd as they looked up at him questioningly, and smiled bravely as he said:

"We must trust the Master. He will have a reason for leaving us at this time. We have only moments left before our Apocalypse. Let us use those wisely to comfort each other in stories of renewed hope."

Chapter Thirteen: Sala'am

My wonderful world is about to die.

I am the sole pilot of a space transporter designed for one purpose: to carry the hope of new life to a neighbouring planet. There is limited space for me as the pilot.

Our engineers have ensured that every available micron of my vessel fulfils its purpose: whether to house the generators that must sustain my cryogenic chambers for at least 1 billion years, or for storage of the precious DNA that is the first part of the legacy of my people.

They nearly forgot to include sufficient room for me but I was insistent that this ship must be manned and that I would take the task of ensuring the placement of our gift on the Planet Earth. I will not risk this most important task to anyone else nor to any computer programme.

First, I must make the trip to Pallas to deposit the second part of our legacy: the collection of our stories. I freely admit, I do not know what to make of these.

The *story feste* began as my 'noble distraction' - the means to prevent my people from falling from grace: my antidote to the predicted changes in our collective behaviour that the stress of impending catastrophe might influence and encourage. My expectations were as Ptere'an's: to see stories of heroism and the fantastical (indeed the cask I commissioned reflects this in the designs of dragons and other mythical creatures on its outer casement). *"Stodge"* he once said and that was what I had anticipated.

Instead, I have eleven stories that speak of our philosophical approach to life, rather than reflect the vividness of our imagination. I am indeed blessed by Ptere'an for he has created a different legacy for our people and one that is as important to me now as the first. I did not plan this but I welcome the gentle message within the stories that our tolerance and respect is something we chose in the face of impossible conflict.

Looking down on Mnesis, its crimson seas and blue grass plains, its ice-topped east pole and mountainous northern ranges, its many cascading falls and white-sanded desert plains, clear dark water lakes and dense uncharted, verdant forests, I cannot resist saying a fond farewell to its beauty. It has been my home for just over thirty years.

My story is as much about my planet as it is about myself. My love of Mnesis is such that I cannot separate the two in my own mind. I am Mnesis and Mnesis is me.

My people have always assumed I am of humble origins and I did not wish to disavow them of this impression. The reality is that my parents are wealthy and that I was born in one of the more exclusive mansions besides the *Clearwater*. I was fortunate to be educated by some of the leading Lectors of the day and was always sidelined to become a Lector myself, through both my aptitude but also through the influence of my parents' wealth.

For those not familiar with our society, I shall briefly explain:

Despite our mutual tolerance and respect for each other, as a people we are also bound by the concept of *status and standing*. In the main, we have become a meritocracy, with the greatest respect being given to those who lead our programmes: engineering, medicine, antiquities, literature, and the natural sciences. Of these, literature is of the highest standing of all, with five thousand appointed Lectors (those who have displayed a special talent in public speaking) acting as our Ruling Council and from whom a Master can be elected to resolve any world challenging conundrum.

Next, we have the Guilds, such as the Tentmakers or Brewers. The seniority of each depends on two things: when they were established (with the oldest Guilds having much greater status than those newly founded), but also, the location of each Guild's Hall or Temple: the nearer to the *Bibliotechnaoi* or the *Forum*, the greater the respect given to a Guild and its membership. Guildmasters carry almost as much respect amongst our people as Lectors.

The third strata amongst our society are the Executives or Directors of the many trades on Mnesis, ranging from crop production, hospitality and retail to technology, mining and fuel production. Every one is a cooperative with the Directors appointed from within the workforce based on an assessment of their skills to set future direction, manage the quality of the product or service and support their customers.

Until the arrival of the disciples, however, wealth (or more accurately the acquisition of material things that demonstrated a long and continuous period over several generations of the same family having held positions of influence and standing within our society) had increasingly begun to take precedence over ability. Families clung to positions of power or influence and sought to pass these down to their children. By the time of my "election" to the post of Lector on my twenty-first birthday, over half my fellow Lectors had inherited their position rather than earned it ... and that alas included me.

One of my first tasks as Lector was to conduct the annual review of our legislation. This was a task always given to the newest Lectors as it was quite meaningless. Apart from a few academic commentaries, no-one had seriously studied our laws in centuries. Indeed, we cannot remember who wrote them or why they would think to do so. Since no-one knew them and we have no-one to enforce them, nor any system of correction in place, our laws are there as a worthy but rather dull piece of fiction. Their review usually involves ensuring that no-one has accidentally deleted them.

Our economy is mainly based upon a system of barter, but coinage developed two centuries ago in the cities, principally because the number of deals being done in each day was so many that people began to lose count of what they had promised or accepted and so coins became the representation of what had been agreed. In the less populous villages and desert plains, coins are still rarely seen and trade continues to be based on the transfer of goods or the offer and promise of future services. Our word is our bond in all such things.

Shaa'mesh's arrival in *Paraclemos* would see the concept of barter and exchange return once more to our cities, especially as our impending doom saw confidence in the value of our coinage collapse. The dancing and singing of the disciples became so popular that they could have charged any price for the pleasure of seeing their happiness, but all my disciples were interested in was their daily bread and this taught the whole of our society a valuable lesson regarding the priority to be given to material things.

I digress. Perhaps, I am afraid of what I must say and am sub-consciously putting off the inevitable? Certainly, I need to remain more focused in the hours ahead as my task must be accomplished without deviation.

I wish to reflect briefly on the loss of Shaa'shesh, made all the more poignant because the Founder's studies of her indicate that her creativity could have sustained her being beyond the four billion years needed to establish new life on Earth. Knowing the girl, as I do, the concept of four billion years without the company of people or trees would have been hell for her. If her beliefs are correct, she is now in the joyful company of HE (or SHE) who has guided the girl's every action since birth, and doubtless the Composer is struggling to get a word in edgewise in their laughing conversation!

Shaa'shesh's evolution is the third part of the legacy of our people.

N'tew was wrong to say she had become something else or 'something different'. She released the talents that sit within all of us; it is merely those talents are suppressed by other distractions such as a quest for status and material things, or by emotions such as anger and hatred.

The Founder has shown that to boost our talents into operancy, we need the catalyst of a conflict coupled with a natural empathy towards our surroundings and our neighbours, uncluttered by worldly things, or those emotions which place us at a distance from our peers. We need to choose harmony and peace in the face of impending tragedy; to turn the other cheek unresistingly; to have complete faith in our world and each other.

The Founder intrigues me. His final e-message to me suggests he has no intention of remaining on our planet for the last moments of its destruction. His forecasts and predictions have been so accurate that I am convinced he is clairvoyant and that his programme to find those who would evolve is partly influenced by his own latent abilities having already become active. His mindset is such that the prospect of four billion years of solitude, stewarding and nurturing future life on Earth, might actually be attractive to him. He asked me for a copy of our stories, which I gladly attached to my reply to him. To which he said that they 'might come in useful one day'.

Six years ago, I sought election as Master. The conundrum posed for the Master on this occasion was: *to find a way for our people to survive the destruction of our planet.* There was never any thought that we might save the planet itself by destroying or diverting the asteroid that approached us. Our scientists were clear that the destruction of Mnesis would have a long-term beneficial impact on the solar system of which we were a part, and thus we agreed to the *Sacrifice of Mnesis*.

Our election process is simple: every Lector is invited to put forward their statement of intent as Master and then the whole population of our planet over the age of sixteen summers, nearly one million people, has the opportunity to elect a Master from the 5000 Lectors. Some of the statements for this election were over twenty thousand words; all were several pages in length as a minimum ... save mine:

"I will listen and I will do my best"

94% of our electorate voted for me. This was the largest proportionate vote in our history and the most overwhelming level of support ever given to a Master. That was truly humbling.

The briefing I received on my election as Master was starkly devoid of hope, however. If *despair* had been something I had the misfortune to experience then I can see I would have readily succumbed.

Collision with the asteroid approaching us could have been but was not to be avoided if the Planet Earth was to survive. Destruction of our planet was therefore essential. Destroying the asteroid would not protect us from a second and larger body hurtling towards us which we could see some 1.2 million years away. It would also see our sister planet destroyed by another asteroid that would strike the Earth in less than a million years from now.

Survival in space was possible for a few centuries at most, but, we would be without a home, and with this limited hope being offered to less than one per cent of our people.

Our scientists had also done studies on our people's reaction to the impending crisis. The first signs of stress-related behaviour were already evident amongst our most vulnerable, especially amongst parents frightened for their young. Our anthropologists predicted the rise of the emotion called 'anger'; they even foresaw violent acts between members of our community.

I remember that I shuddered at this last thought, but then realised that my role was not to shun away from such terrible concepts but rather to find an answer that either prevented this from happening or at the very least mitigated the damage to our race's psyche that such a fall from grace might cause.

Then the scientists came to me with the news that their many thousands of studies of our sister planet had revealed no evidence of the specialist proteins called *Introns* needed to act as the catalyst and the codebook for the creation of both strands of RiboNucleic Acid, and then their descendant and more complex, double stranded DeoxyriboNucleic Acid.

Proteins, amino and nucleic acids had been found in abundance, but several million years of evolution had seen no bonding, no strings holding molecular particles, no sign of combination covalence to form the two types of array needed to create the unique double-helix of DNA and, equally importantly, no evidence of self-replication.

We were bravely facing the annihilation of our planet for no discernible purpose or benefit: the hope of sentient life on Earth just simply did not exist.

I remember that I laughed at the impossibility of the task being presented to me ... and yet the faith my people had in me gave me the confidence I needed to continue to quest for an answer. My self-confidence was then given a significant boost when one day I met Shaa'shesh, climbing a tree as usual, and she called down to me: "You are the Master, and any answer you conceive shall be the right one. Have no fear in yourself but believe!"

With the return of my self-belief came my solution and it was in three parts: first, to find an immediate goal to bind our people together in pride and harmony. Thus our people could make the *choice* to be peaceful when faced with the end of our world, despite a predilection to violence as shown by Ptere'an's assault of Shaa'shesh. This example of choosing harmony over conflict under the most stressful of circumstances would be captured in a selection of our stories.

The second and third parts of my answer I kept secret for fear that others would prevent my intended course. Our sister planet needed a source of proteins with the right code to inspire the nucleic acids on Earth to join and replicate ... **and the people of Mnesis were to be that source**. Our genes, our nucleic acid, our proteins, our amino acids, our *Introns* could become the basis of sentient life on our neighbouring world. Those genes would also include the potential for telepathy, telekinesis, clairvoyance and clairaudience in future generations, if the experiments of the Founder and Shaa'shesh's concept of *faith* were to prove true.

For the two years before my Address in the *Bibliotechnaoi,* the scientists on Mnesis collected our genome from every corner of my planet, stored it within the sealed chambers of the newly commissioned space ship *Evolution*, and began to programme the ship with one purpose: a single manned mission to plunge into the centre of the Planet Earth.

Disaster briefly struck, when we discovered that a virus had begun to kill our population in its final weeks and had almost certainly entered into the gene pool we had gathered over years as part of The Genome Project.

Shaa'shesh understood what was required, of course, and gave her own unique blood that we might all be remembered. Not only through the nobility of our end, but through the *Introns* that we shall give to the newly forming world that is our neighbour, the foundation and building blocks for its future, made free from the risk of a genetically disabling disease by one girl's sacrifice, and now to take its chance to evolve on the Planet Earth, which is my ultimate destination.

In the final moments of her life, she also demonstrated the evolutionary potential of humankind to develop powers of telepathy, telekenesis, clairvoyance and many other similar mental abilities. Her sacrifice ensured that this potential will become part of the gift of the people of Mnesis.

There are no traces of life on Earth yet ... but there will be.

My gift to my world is that our genetic imprint shall be the basis of sentient life **on a new world** – it may take one billion years before Earth is ready for our *Introns* to survive and four billion years before sentient life itself shall evolve, but today I start a process of evolution that will see our race return in the millennia to come, born on a new world, and kept safe by a protective curtain of asteroids, being the last remains of Mnesis and the sacrifice made willingly by my gentle people.

In time, I hope that the stories we have told will mould the value set of a new race into the image of our own and that the people of Earth will find their true path to peace, respect and tolerance, *The Way* that we once we trod.

On Earth I pray that our ancestors will learn, as we did, to turn their backs on hatred, contempt, anger and intolerance to choose instead the path to peace, respect and restraint. For these, our stories, were never about our past; they were always written for our future on the Planet Earth ..."

There is an ancient dream of a great writer, once held in captivity on the small island of Patmos by a foreign oppressor, which opens with the following words:

"In the beginning was the message ..."

That message was a series of simple stories of how life can be conducted in peaceful co-existence through love, kindness, compassion and charity. We are told that this dream of paradise was sealed by his closest friend, generously sacrificing his own life to open the way to a new world beyond all death. We can still choose to live their dream, **whenever or *however it is told.*** *Above all, we are called to remember the story of one man's sacrifice (the AnaMnesis that is the foundation of so many faiths)*

The Founder

Alsharah o Altalic

Dear Reader, this is the serious bit!

I hope you enjoy reading these stories without the need for any genuinely serious contemplation, commentary or explanation. If you feel the urge to read this Altalic then you are taking this book far too seriously and probably need to follow Shaa'shesh's example: do not think, just take the plunge.

If Ptere'an were here, doubtless he would describe my Alsharah as 'stodge', whilst Shaa'shesh would roll over with a fit of the giggles at my pomposity.

This book is meant to be fun because humour, and the joy it brings, is one of Allah's greatest gifts, lifting the spirit as well as opening our hearts to the warmth of his love.

There is a difference between humour, however, and irreverence. The difference is love and respect for the subject-matter. Shemer would discover this when she was to learn that tricks are not always kind.

This book is written out of a deep sense of love for the traditions of Islam, Christianity and Judaism. Arabic is a beautifully poetic language and its prayers are the music of my soul. The traditions of Sufi embrace respect for all of Allah's creation, including people, the natural world and the environment. Protecting and respecting **all** life is an important part of demonstrating that we are qualified to be the caretakers of Allah's creation when we take our place in Paradise.

This book offers a re-telling of stories that will be familiar to those from most faiths but written as perhaps they might be told around the camp fires in the desert by those brought up in the verbal tradition of passing on their beliefs. Many of these short stories are also based on true happenings; they are the tales of friends or stories taken from the media of today. I am grateful to my friends for their love, companionship and insight. Numa'mesh's recipe is genuine; the Pericope of Oroma, the stories of Shemer, Asostos and M'tew, Bart'lmew and Nar'csa are based on the real experiences of friends, and the concept of *Introns* is a few years old now.

The Revelation of the Sea gets a mention and is one of the oldest mystical dreams from Islam. *The Revelation of the Sea* teaches us that true salvation is through trusting in the love of Allah by following the purity of our *hearts'* calling and his love.

I most humbly apologise for some of the word-play in the naming of characters, places and chapters. For those who enjoy a puzzle, there are puns to decipher; for those of us just looking for a story and nothing deeper than that, work on the basis that the Mnemonic language made its way *genetically* into Latin, Greek, Arabic and Persian, hence so many similarities in the nomenclature I have used.

There are a couple of other references that will be familiar to most people but may confuse the reader if you are not familiar with them:

The "Eagle of Patmos", the prisoner kept captive by a foreign oppressor, is a reference to the captivity of St John, the Gospel writer, who used 'Word' as a metaphor for God but also to reflect the importance of The Message given by God's son. He was kept prisoner on Patmos by the Emperors of Rome.

The naming of the Planet as Mnesis is a shortening of the term for the Eucharistic sacrifice ('**Anamnesis**') or the sacrifice Christians celebrate at the heart of their Weekly Service of Worship, being the gift by Christ of his body, blood and finally his life.

I make no apology that some of the philosophy by which the gentle people of Mnesis live is based loosely on the Sufi tradition – it is a value-set with which I am familiar, and I hope no-one will condemn me for wishing with all my heart, mind and soul that my child and child's children will be allowed to grow up in a world free from war, terror and violence. Let us hope that we can make **the right choice** regarding how we live our loves peacefully, in love and respect for each other as the people of Mnesis did.

With all my love and prayers,

Layla Ghaniyah Abrar

"Here is the House of Layla:

I walk beneath her silent tower
Kiss the clematis on her walls
Touch the trellis where wisteria falls
But it is not love for her walls
To which my beating heart calls
SHE is the source of my desire"

(Layla o Majnan, from the orig. Quintet by Nizami Gandavi, modern trans. by Sleeping Dragon)

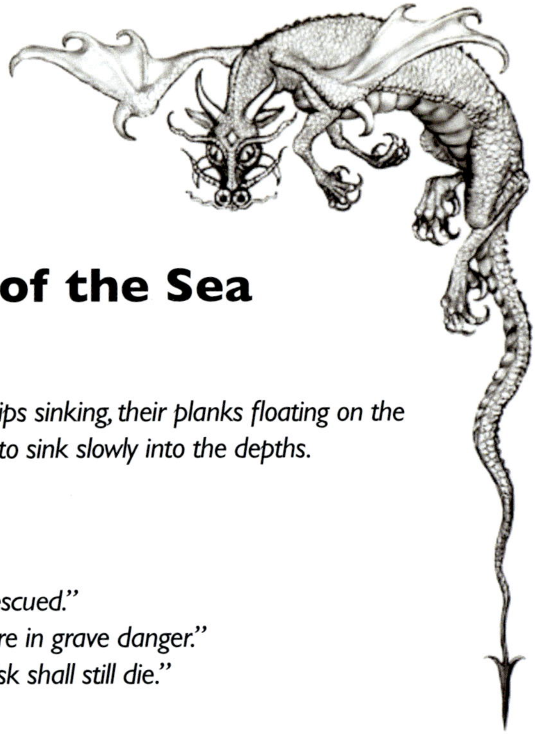

The Revelation of the Sea

"Look! There is the Sea" and I saw ships sinking, their planks floating on the surface. Then the planks also began to sink slowly into the depths.

And I could see that:

"Those who sailed in the ships would not be rescued."
"Those who threw themselves into the Sea were in grave danger."
"Those who sailed another way and took no risk shall still die."

"Only when we take risks and challenge the material world can we be saved."

"The surface of the Sea is shining bright but this is a light that cannot be reached."
"The bottom of the Sea is impenetrable darkness and also cannot be reached."

"Between the two are ferocious dragons!"

"Do not swim beaneath the surface of the Sea for you will be blinded by the ship's shadow."
"If you fall into the Sea or stay on your ship, you shall be eaten by the dragons."

"In the Sea there are many different currents: which shall carry you to safety?"

"I deceive you if I say that anything can save you ... except me!"
"If you die for any other cause except to have followed me, then you shall be lost in the Sea."

"This world belongs to those who turn their back on me
... the next world belongs to those who fish in the Sea to save my people for me."

(Modern translation by Sleeping Dragon)

If you enjoyed this book, you may be interested in the following by the same author:

Fantasy and science fiction

The Adventures of the half-elf and cyborg, Cymbeline, dragon-rider, duchess of Fearnost and the last to believe in God:

The Servers Soul

Suspended Belief

Roaring Flamebringer then returns in:

An Audience with the Sleeping Dragon

The Rise of Clan Faeron, the Chronicles of Serena, Element of the Air and Empress of Atlantis:

Alanaa, the Water Element

From the Ashes of Despair

The Persian and Jovan Wars

Paradise Found

The World of RETHA

Detective novels

The Westerfield Mysteries

Truer than Truth

Short stories and poetry

Tales from the Burning Bush